CANDLELIGHT

Supreme

"WHY DID YOU RUN AWAY FROM MEXICO?" REID DEMANDED.

"I told you I had to leave soon, that my vacation was almost over," Mari countered.

"You had two days left."

She forced herself to look him in the eye. "I chose to leave when I did for reasons of my own."

"What reasons?"

"Reid, we had a very nice time in Mexico, but there were no promises made on either side," she began softly, gearing herself for the hardest speech she would ever make—because it was all a lie. "And now I'm back where I belong and you should be back where you belong."

"Basically, you're saying we indulged in nothing more than a one-night stand," he stated bluntly. "Lady, you should be in Hollywood; you're a great actress. Now, how about the truth, for a change?"

CANDLELIGHT SUPREMES

QUANTITY SALES

Most Dell Books are available at special quantity discounts when purchased in bulk by corporations, organizations, and special-interest groups. Custom imprinting or excerpting can also be done to fit special needs. For details write: Dell Publishing Co., Inc., 1 Dag Hammarskjold Plaza, New York, NY 10017, Attn.: Special Sales Dept., or phone: (212) 605-3319.

INDIVIDUAL SALES

Are there any Dell Books you want but cannot find in your local stores? If so, you can order them directly from us. You can get any Dell book in print. Simply include the book's title, author, and ISBN number, if you have it, along with a check or money order (no cash can be accepted) for the full retail price plus 75¢ per copy to cover shipping and handling. Mail to: Dell Readers Service, Dept. FM, 6 Regent Street, Livingston, N.J. 07039.

A PERILOUS AFFAIR

Linda Randall Wisdom

A CANDLELIGHT SUPREME

Published by
Dell Publishing Co., Inc.
1 Dag Hammarskjold Plaza
New York, New York 10017

ISBN: 0-440-16868-6

Printed in the United States of America

June 1987

10 9 8 7 6 5 4 3 2 1

WFH

To Our Readers:

We are pleased and excited by your overwhelmingly positive response to our Candlelight Supremes. Unlike all the other series, the Supremes are filled with more passion, adventure, and intrigue, and are obviously the stories you like best.

In months to come we will continue to publish books by many of your favorite authors as well as the very finest work from new authors of romantic fiction. As always, we are striving to present unique, absorbing love stories —the very best love has to offer.

Breathtaking and unforgettable, Supremes follow in the great romantic tradition you've come to expect *only* from Candlelight Romances.

Your suggestions and comments are always welcome. Please let us hear from you.

Sincerely,

The Editors
Candlelight Romances
1 Dag Hammarskjold Plaza
New York, New York 10017

A PERILOUS
AFFAIR

PROLOGUE

Pain . . . waves of hot, breath-stealing pain began at her toes and traveled upward to the top of her head. And her face—every nerve ending from her forehead to her chin screamed out in agony for relief. She sensed an IV needle stuck in her arm so why didn't someone give her something for the pain? Didn't they realize how much she hurt? She wanted to tell them but couldn't seem to open her mouth. The same was true with opening her eyes, the effort was too great for her weakened body. At least it didn't hurt to hear what was going on around her. Did they know she was awake? She wished she could tell them. She must be in a hospital somewhere; hospital sheets always felt scratchy against her sensitive skin.

"Is she going to make it?" The man's voice sounded familiar, not that of a relative or close friend, just a voice she remembered from another life.

"To be honest with you, it will be a miracle if she survives the night." That had to be a doctor speaking. They always sound as if they know what's going to happen before it does. How wonderful to hear oneself described in such cold, clinical terms. If it didn't hurt so much she'd laugh and really give them a scare. "Both cheekbones have been broken along with her nose and jaw. She's on the verge of starvation and it's going to take every bit of willpower she has to make it past the first critical twelve hours. I'd also like several photographs of the way she used to look so the plastic surgeon can study them, if she does happen to make it."

"Hmm." The man didn't seem to have anything to say about that. He had a picture of her, she was sure. "We'll discuss that later."

There was so much she felt she had to tell him. Things and events she didn't want to remember, but her sense of duty told her she had to recall everything no matter how much it hurt. There were flashbacks that sent her whimpering in fear. Harsh guttural voices shouting at her, demanding something she didn't have or know about, hurting her, closing her up in dark places. It was all so frightening! No, she didn't want to remember it any more. If she let it slip from her mind she wouldn't hurt any more. Ah, that was much better.

A loud voice, this one even more familiar, sounded nearby, but not in the same room. She had to see him . . . talk to him, but she couldn't move or speak. He would make it all better, she knew he would. Something from deep inside of her flickered to life, demanding escape, but she was too weak to allow it to happen.

"Let me take care of this," the man standing near her bed said crisply. "Then we'll decide how to handle her." A door clicked shut a moment later.

Reid was angry—correction, he was past angry and well on his way to becoming furious. Why wasn't he allowed in to see her? What was going on in there?

"I don't give a damn what anyone says. I want to see her now!" he demanded of the terrified nurse who vainly tried to placate him. "And no one is going to stop me from going in there, do you understand me?"

"Reid." The quiet voice held a command rarely argued with, but Reid was past listening to anyone's orders.

Reid spun around, his deep-gray eyes alive with his rage. "Where is Alicia, Lucas? You're not going to keep me from her. You had to go ahead and play God with our lives, and look what happened; you almost got her killed! I want to see Alicia and you're not going to stop me."

Lucas was a nondescript man who blended easily into any background even though the power he held surrounded him like a dark cloak.

"You shouldn't be here, Reid," he chided. "I wanted to see your report on that crisis so I could read it over the weekend. In fact, I didn't expect to see you back from Yugoslavia for another week or so."

Reid's six-two frame towered over the smaller man. "I'm sure you were hoping I wouldn't be back so soon. Let me tell you now, I'm not leaving until I see Alicia." His deep gravelly voice carried a threat he'd gladly carry out.

"Then you can just go on home, write up your report, and get back to Yugoslavia on the next flight because she died ten minutes ago without regaining consciousness."

Reid's normally bronzed skin turned paper white, his dark eyes stark with the pain.

"No," he whispered harshly, clenching his hands and releasing them to relieve the tension moving through his body. *"No!* She is not dead!" He covered his face with his hands, refusing to believe what he had just heard.

Beeping sounds surrounded her. She heard the low murmur of a man's voice then a woman answering. Suddenly the entire room vibrated with a sound beginning like a low moan and rising to the howling rage of a wild animal in agony. She wanted to question the origin of the sound since she could finally open her mouth without hurting too much, but clouds began to gather in her brain and she slipped into a dark oblivion as the medication that had been slipped into her IV entered her bloodstream.

CHAPTER ONE

It had been a longer day than usual for Mari. How she hated the end of the month when getting her books together for her accountant had to be her top priority. Hopefully, they would be in better order than last month. She shouldn't complain. After all, that's what happens when you become a successful businesswoman, she told herself as she let herself into her brick home on the outskirts of Charlotte. She wandered upstairs to change out of her peach linen two-piece dress and into a blue-and-silver striped leotard and silver tights. Following a now time-honored custom, she ascended the stairs to the third floor, which housed an incredible amount of exercise equipment, one of the reasons she had bought the house. For the next hour she worked out until her body was dripping with sweat and her mind was a pleasurable blank. Even though three of the four walls were mirrored she didn't look at her reflection once.

Back in her bedroom an hour later Mari showered, changed into a misty-green cotton caftan, and wandered downstairs to fix herself dinner.

If she cared to stop to think about it she would

have realized that this evening was a repetition of the night before and so on. She didn't care to delve too far back into the past—it wasn't allowed.

As she did so many of the other nights she spent alone, Mari read, watched a little television, undressed, and went to bed.

As usual Mari woke up in the middle of the night with her body bathed in a cold sweat, her eyes dilated with fear. Guttural voices from the past echoed inside her head demanding things she didn't know or couldn't remember. She immediately looked toward the dresser where an Art Deco night-light brightened the darkness with a soft glow. She inhaled deeply and let it out slowly to calm her racing heart. It had been almost three years and still the dreams invaded her sleep.

In one convulsive movement, she pushed the covers aside and jumped out of bed, making a beeline to the bathroom. There the light was bright and harsh, beating down on her pale features as she stared at her reflection in the mirror.

Golden-brown hair that was usually feathered back was now plastered to her damp scalp. Green eyes were bright against parchment skin.

She took inventory: rounded eyes, a button nose, a mouth that would have been kissable under other circumstances, a strong jaw. But that wasn't what she expected to see in the mirror. The woman remembered had long blond streaked hair, deep purple eyes, slim features, an easy smile. She braced her hands against the cold porcelain sink.

"No!" she almost hissed, putting her face to the

14

mirror until her breath fogged the slick surface. "I am still me. *I am still me,*" she maintained between clenched teeth. "And no one can take that away from me. *No one!*"

It was a routine she should have been used to. The nightmare, the compulsive need to remember who she used to be, even though that person had been declared officially dead. Alicia Brookes had been "buried" in a cemetery in Somerset, England, while Mari Chandler was alive and well in Charlotte, North Carolina.

Alicia, one of the top agents for an international agency in Washington, D.C., had died as a result of the injuries she incurred during incarceration in a Middle East prison, and Mari had been born. Leaving the agency didn't hurt as much as knowing she would never be able to see her family and friends again. Not to mention the man she had loved more than life itself.

Reid; her heart and body still ached for him. She doubted she'd ever get over him. That was part of the deal though. When you take up a new life, you have to give up the old one. But giving up something dear to you doesn't make you forget.

While everyone in Charlotte knew her as Mari Chandler, owner of Naughty and Nice, an exclusive lingerie boutique, she couldn't help but remember the name she was given at birth—Alicia Ashley-Brookes, daughter of a well-to-do London businessman.

Everything had always been a game to Alicia. She breezed through school, graduating with honors, and with her flair for languages decided to apply for the foreign service. Before she went through with her plan an international agency few people had heard of approached her, saying her skills as a linguist and her contacts with the jet set would come in handy. After extensive training she was sent out into the field with one of their top agents, Reid Morgan. From the beginning she was fascinated with the not good-looking but incredibly sexy and intense man who furthered her training in infiltration, picking locks, and every other little trick a good spy should know.

For four years they had worked as the perfect team with no sexual overtones, at least none they had dared to acknowledge. Then it all changed. Mari couldn't remember exactly how it started. She did remember the night they had drunk wine at a little café in Budapest and how an electric current flowed between them as they sat there and talked and drank. When they returned to their hotel they only used one room and one bed. Their heated affair continued for over a year without their work suffering. Who knows how long it would have gone on if they hadn't committed the unpardonable sin within the agency—they declared their plans to retire and marry.

Lucas, the director, had been determined not to lose his two best agents. In order to ensure his wishes, he split them up and sent Alicia on a mission to a troubled small Middle Eastern country. To get her to go he had promised not to stand in their way if she would take this mission for him. Her cover was blown almost immediately and she was thrown into prison.

It had been eight hellish months before Alicia was rescued by a group of freedom fighters. They bombed the prison and released many of their comrades. She had been in such poor physical shape she had had to be carried out of the prison on a stretcher. Lucas had been notified and he had her flown out immediately. She was returned to the United States a broken woman, both physically and emotionally. For more months than she cared to remember, she lived with pain as her mind healed and her broken body was repaired by a skilled team of surgeons. Her new face was a great shock to her but what was worse was when Lucas, in his blunt way, told her that there were those who were convinced she knew about the terrorist network they had set up and wanted her dead. The trouble was that she wanted to remember nothing of those months spent in a dark and dank hole next door to hell, so if she did indeed know about it, the information was locked away in the dark recesses of her memory. These people would do anything, including destroy those close to her, to get to her, Lucas insisted. Her best bet was to allow Alicia to die and take up a new life. She had no idea that Lucas had told Reid months earlier that she was dead. All she knew was that Reid hadn't come to see her during her convalescence and Lucas's excuses that he was on assignment didn't ring quite true until the day Lucas told her the truth—that she was dead to all who knew her.

She had listened to Lucas tell her there could be no contact with anyone from her past. The old

Alicia would have told the man what he could do with his suggestion, but the new one was a broken woman and feared the worst for her family and her lover. While she knew Reid could take care of himself, he couldn't be on guard twenty-four hours a day, and she wouldn't have been able to live with his death on her hands. Nursing a broken heart that she knew would never mend, she recuperated in an out-of-the-way house in Virginia and worked hard at turning into Mari Chandler. The blond streaks were removed from her hair, extended-wear contact lenses changed the color of her eyes, and elocution lessons replaced the crisp British accent with a slower Southern drawl. The plastic surgeon had already altered her features so drastically that no one would have recognized her even at close range. Mari/Alicia did a thorough job, practicing for hours until she could write with her left hand instead of her right, ruthlessly changing all of her Alicia habits and developing new ones. Then her superiors assisted her in finding a new place to live and opening her shop. With her new background already set up, Mari Chandler settled in quite nicely. She might even have forgotten all about her previous life if it weren't for the nightmares that she had six nights out of seven and her inability to sleep in a completely dark room. She once joked to Lucas that she was a burned-out agent sent out to pasture, but deep down she always felt there was something he wasn't telling her behind the work involved in her makeover. Her main regret was never seeing Reid again and not knowing if he were alive or dead.

Over the years she hadn't dared bring up Reid's name to Lucas, and Lucas never breathed a word.

A bitter smile touched her lips. She was certain someone from the agency kept an eye on her from time to time. Lucas had told her that he hated losing such a valuable agent, but he also had to admit that in her present frame of mind she was no good to him. Besides, Mari Chandler wasn't the kind of woman who would work as a *spy*. She was the kind who would be happy running her shop and eventually marrying a nice man and starting a family.

Mari had dated in the past year or so but no man sparked her interest. She knew she was going to have to exorcise Reid from her soul if she wanted to remain sane. Time alone would not accomplish that, she realized now. After wiping her flushed face with a cool damp cloth she returned to bed, but sleep eluded her until dawn crept into her room.

Mari went to her store an hour early that morning to try to catch up on some of the paperwork.

The two-story Victorian house where her shop was located was her pride and joy. Painted a pale yellow with white trim, white lace curtains framed a demure white silk and lace peignoir set in the front bay window. The simple display brought in many browsers who soon turned into buyers.

Mari's merchandise was expensive, much of it imported and handmade, but no one ever complained about the exorbitant prices. She had always reveled in the feel of fine silks and cotton against her bare skin and knew other women felt the same way. Her many clients were proof of that. In fact, Mari's shop was doing so well she toyed with the idea of opening a second store in Charleston by the end of the year.

Mari stared down at her ledgers but didn't see the black inked numbers that usually gave her so much pleasure. Without thinking she doodled on a sheet of notepaper. When her eyes fell to the paper, they widened in shock at the harsh-visaged male features staring up at her. She swiftly crumpled the sheet, hunted for the packet of matches she kept in her desk drawer, and burned the offending article.

By the time Denise, her assistant, showed up, Mari still hadn't accomplished a thing.

"Well, I see we're hard at work again," Denise said sarcastically, standing in the office doorway, her hands braced on her hips. With her blue-black hair caught up in an intricate twist at the back of her head and a red silk dress hugging her slim curves, she resembled an exotic bird. "I ran into Ed outside. Our shipment from Loré arrived so I thought I would unpack the boxes while you watch the store."

"Are you sure I'm the boss and you're the employee?" Mari asked dryly, leaning back in her chair.

"Of course. Anytime someone comes in and demands to speak to the boss, don't I point you out?"

Mari rolled her eyes. "You're really good at that when they're someone I would rather not speak to."

Denise walked into the office while digging

deep into the large black leather purse she carried. She tossed a handful of folded papers onto Mari's desk. Mari reached out and picked up the brochures.

"Is this your way of asking me if you can take your vacation early this year?"

Denise groaned loudly. "Mari, I swear you're impossible! These are for you." She flicked one with a scarlet-tipped nail.

She shook her head. "I don't need a vacation, Denise. Besides, there's too much to do around here."

This time Denise rolled her eyes. "As owner, you have the right to take a break any time you want to. Besides, when was the last time you took a real vacation and not just a long weekend? I bet you can't even remember."

Oh, she could remember, all right. It had been at that lovely resort in Mexico she and Reid had stolen away to after their last assignment together. She could remember every beautiful hour of it, especially the time spent in bungalow 12. But she wasn't allowed to remember those days because those memories didn't rightfully belong to Mari Chandler.

"Mari, are you all right?" Denise asked with concern, seeing the dark look enter her boss's eyes.

She managed to smile and nod. "Sure, I'm fine. I made the mistake of coming in early hoping to get the end-of-the-month paperwork out of the way and didn't get one thing accomplished."

"You never do." Denise perched her hip on the

desk edge. "You need to get away for a while, Mari," she said softly. "You spend practically all your waking hours in this place. You've probably gone on two dates in the past six months."

"And look what disasters they turned out to be!" Mari tried to inject laughter into a conversation that was turning much too serious for her liking. "One decided not to 'call on me' again because his mother thought it was unseemly that I owned a shop that sold undergarments. And the other, well, he's also better forgotten. I'm just not cut out to date." She knew Alicia would have handled both situations with her usual aplomb. Funny, she always thought of Alicia as another person, as someone she had known a long time ago.

"If you'd just go barhopping with me a few times you'd soon learn different," Denise coaxed. "Honey, there are some men in town who'd make your head spin."

Mari sincerely doubted that. She looked at her friend's face and recognized the avid look in her eye. Denise was determined to either get Mari away on a vacation or find her a man. Of the two, Mari preferred the vacation.

Denise looked up, her head cocked to one side as melodic chimes of the old-fashioned wall clock filled the room.

"Opening time," she announced, hopping off the desk. "You look over those brochures and figure out where you're going."

"Aren't you afraid I'll choose a dud?" Mari teased, fanning them out like a deck of cards.

"No chance. I selected these very carefully. If

you're going away I wanted to make sure you'd be someplace where you had a good chance of meeting men." Denise raised her eyebrows comically.

"You better go unlock the front door."

"Tell me as soon as you've decided where you're going."

"I'll unpack the Loré shipment first."

Denise's face fell. Mari knew how much her employee enjoyed inspecting the new lingerie and putting aside anything she liked. Mari always teased her, saying she was Naughty and Nice's best customer.

"Go," Mari told her, finding it hard to keep a smile from curving her lips.

"The Caribbean is nice this time of year," Denise sang out over her shoulder as she sashayed out to the shop floor. "So is Australia. And I hear the men outnumber the women Down Under! Hmm, on second thought maybe I'll go myself."

Mari pushed her fingers through her hair. She listened to the familiar sounds of Denise unlatching the front door, sending the tiny brass bells that hung over it tinkling, then the ring of the cash drawer opening as Denise checked the contents.

"We're going to need dimes and nickels before the day is out," Denise called out.

"I have to go to the bank this morning. I'll pick some up then," Mari replied, closing the ledgers. She would take them home with her that evening and work on them after dinner. She scanned the brochures, then halted at the fourth and dropped the others to read it more thoroughly.

Isle of Heaven. Reid had said it was the most

beautiful place on earth. The two weeks they had spent there had been very special. The brochure spoke of the amenities—white sandy beach, horseback riding, scuba diving, and tennis. Helicopter service to Mexico City. A perfect place for lovers, it was dubbed. How well she knew!

It was a sign! she decided, reading every word. What better place to exorcise Reid from her heart than by returning to the last place where they had reconfirmed their love? She studied the brochure and decided to stop by the travel agency on the way to the bank.

Why did D.C. have to be so damn hot? Reid grumbled to himself as he unlocked the door to the small boxlike apartment he called home. Once inside, he set the canvas flight bag on the floor then fumbled for the air-conditioner controls and turned the blower on high. He picked the bag up again and walked into the bedroom. It was even hotter in there and smelled musty from six months of disuse.

He should call Lucas, but he wasn't ready to talk to him just yet. He stripped off his clothing and walked into the bathroom to turn on the shower. After months of coping with erratic East European plumbing, he was grateful for the steady stream of cool water that shot out of the faucet. Fifteen minutes later he felt cooler and more able to cope with the debriefing ahead. When that was over he was going to ask for time off. He looked in the mirror as he towel-dried his dark-auburn hair that was peppered with gray. Dark circles and

24

bloodshot eyes were a reminder that he hadn't had a good night's sleep in more than two weeks. Walking naked back into the bedroom, he was glad to feel the cooler air circulating in the room. Thank God for air conditioning!

As he unpacked his dirty clothing Reid thought about where to take his well-earned vacation. Roughing it in Canada sounded tempting, but after roughing it in East Germany, he'd had enough of outdoor living. There was Hawaii. Naw, he'd only end up hunting up a few old friends and spending his time in the bars, instead of on the beach. He opened a drawer to get out a clean pair of socks when a picture winked up at him. He froze before slowly reaching out to pick it up. It was a picture of Alicia standing on the beach in Mexico wearing her drop-dead-red bikini. Her pose was sultry, her eyes displayed pure mischief, and she had a come-hither smile. Reid felt the pain claw at his vitals. Even three years later the thought of her still hurt. It was time to do something about it, and the best place was Mexico. After talking to Lucas he would make his reservations. There was no doubt in his mind he would get the time off. After all he'd done for the agency, they could do something for him. He set the picture down very carefully as if it were made of the finest porcelain.

Mari was in a daze as she took a flight to Atlanta, then to Mexico City and from there the tour bus to the resort. She was assaulted by many memories as she listened to the rapid patter in the nearby marketplace and voices of the porters assisting the incoming guests. She smiled automatically to the porter who took her bags and followed him inside to the desk. Still in a daze, she filled out the appropriate forms and extended her American Express card. Her frozen smile didn't waver when the desk clerk told her that yes, bungalow 12 was available for the lovely señorita, and that he hoped she would have a wonderful stay with them. He handed the porter the room key and went on to the next guest.

Mari looked over the spacious lobby decorated in bright blues and greens with an Aztec motif. She was positive the colors had been oranges and gold the last time she was there.

When they reached the bungalow facing the beach, Mari allowed the porter to enter first. She felt herself tensing as she slowly stepped inside. The furniture was natural wicker with blue Aztec print cushions. The bed was king-size with a matching bedspread.

"Thank you," she whispered, tipping the porter and watching him leave. She opened the drapes and the windows. At least the strong smell of the salt air was familiar! She spun around and studied every piece of furniture. Nothing was the same. The bed used to face the window and the couch had been where the bed was now. She wanted to scream her outrage over the changes and stopped herself just in time.

Wait a minute, a little voice told her. *You wanted to break with the past. If you had too many re-*

minders, you might not be able to do so. Now you shouldn't have that problem.

Still, old habits died hard. Just as Alicia used to do every time she entered a hotel room, Mari's eyes swept over the room looking for the slightest discrepancy. She checked every piece of furniture, picked up the lamps and inspected the bottoms and looked inside the shades. Knowing Lucas, she wouldn't have been surprised if he had sent one of his goons down to keep an eye on her. Just because she left the business didn't mean she would be left on her own for the rest of her life. Once her study of the room was finished, she opened her bags and began her unpacking. She decided to have dinner in her room and then make it an early night. She was surprised at how tired she was. Yet Alicia never suffered from jet lag the many times she traveled from one country to another at a moment's notice. Mari shook her head vehemently. No, this was the time to discard all those memories. With that in mind, Mari put her clothes away and went into the bathroom for a much-needed shower to wash away the travel-accumulated grime.

"I was led to believe bungalow twelve was available," Reid commented in a dangerous tone. He was dead tired after three plane changes, only to arrive in Mexico City to learn that the last tour bus had left and that the helicopters didn't fly at night. Nor were there any rental cars available. The taxi driver he finally talked into driving him had to have been a kamikaze pilot in a previous life. Now, in search of some much-needed sleep in a comfortable bed, he was being told that the bungalow he had requested was already taken.

"We are sorry, Señor Morgan, but the clerk you spoke to is new and did not look at our reservation list," the clerk apologized, unable to hold the man's steely gaze.

Reid sighed. He should have realized nothing would be in his favor tonight. "Then what do you have available?"

"Bungalow ten is ready, señor."

He held his hand out for the key. "Fine. I can find my own way."

Five minutes later Reid dropped his duffel bag on the bed wondering how it could have gained twenty pounds since he had packed it that morning. He was so tired he felt ready to drop. He looked out the window in the direction of bungalow 12. Even as tired as he was, he couldn't help wondering why he had been first told the bungalow was available and then suddenly it wasn't. It sounded suspicious. It was all part of the job. Since an agent could never relax his guard, he took the time to look over the room for any unwanted electrical devices. After making sure the room was clean, he felt ready to relax.

He raked his hands through his hair and rubbed one hand over his stubbly jaw. Even though it was late at night a shower and shave might make him feel more human. He wasn't pleased to hear that bungalow 12 was taken but he knew there was nothing he could do about it. Besides, perhaps it was better that he wasn't staying there. It might have been even more difficult to release Alicia from his soul if he slept in the room they had once shared.

He stroked his jaw reflectively and bent over to unzip the bag. Nestled among underwear and jeans were two bottles of Jack Daniel's. He pulled one out, unscrewed the top, and lifted the bottle to his lips. The strong alcohol burned its way down every inch of his throat and landed in a fiery stream in his empty stomach. He didn't hesitate to take a second drink then another.

Reid sat down on the edge of the bed and looked at the black-labeled bottle cradled in his hands. The curse he uttered was self-deprecating and to the point. He brought the bottle to his lips again, waiting for the mind-numbing effect the whiskey would soon bring him.

A half hour later the bottle was empty and he was lost in his dreams of the past.

"Damn you, Alicia!" he ground out, his words slurred. He threw the bottle across the room. "why'd you have to die and leave me?"

Even after all this time, Reid remembered the shock he had felt when Lucas had told him that Alicia was dead. He even refused to allow Reid to see her body. Reid felt that that was the reason he had so much trouble believing she was truly gone. If only he could have been allowed to see her. Then he could have convinced himself that she was dead.

More than three years ago they had flown down here for an idyllic week of loving and sunning. It was during those beautiful days that Reid had proposed to Alicia and she had happily accepted. Ten days later she had been sent to that Middle East hellhole and she had died as a result.

Groaning, Reid lay back on the bed. His insides were in knots and his head spun from all the alcohol he had consumed on an empty stomach. He was contemplating opening the second bottle when he quietly passed out.

Mari awoke just as the sun broke over the horizon. She jumped out of bed and looked outside with eager anticipation.

She dressed in a mint-green terry-cloth jumpsuit and ran outside to the shoreline while it was still unmarred by footprints. It seemed natural that the hotel guests were still sleeping peacefully in their beds while she greeted her first day there.

She ran along the damp packed sand and down into the warm water until it lapped up against her knees.

"It's beautiful!" she shouted happily, dancing around with her arms flung out over her head. "Hello, world, I'm back."

Reid groaned and rolled over. He sat up, holding his head with both hands as if afraid it would shatter at any moment, and tried to work his woolcovered tongue around his mouth, which felt full of sand. Finally he got off the bed and staggered into the bathroom, although his entire body revolted against the movement.

After ducking his head in a sink filled with cold

water, he managed to make his way back into the bedroom.

Reid winced and swore fiercely when the sound of a woman's voice tore through his tender head. He walked over to the window and looked out, his bloodshot eyes seeing the last thing he expected to see.

A woman with golden-brown hair danced on the shore with her arms flung out as if embracing the new day. Her happy laughter brought to mind someone else who had enjoyed dancing on the beach at dawn.

For a moment a hungover and befuddled Reid was convinced he was watching Alicia engage in that same primitive ritual as she had long ago. At the distance, he couldn't make out the woman's features, and he was easily deluded into thinking that he and Alicia had returned to Mexico together. As he breathed her name he knew he had to get a closer look at the unknown woman.

Realizing he had somehow disposed of his clothing sometime during the night, Reid turned to pull on a pair of jeans. He ignored the pain in his head and body as he dressed. He had to get outside before she disappeared with the birth of the new day.

By the time he ran out onto the beach, however, the woman was gone and any footprints she would have made had been washed away by the tide.

Reid spun around, looking for the smallest sign that she had really been there, feeling anger and frustration fill him at not finding any. He began to wonder if she hadn't been an apparition due to his hangover.

He walked slowly back to his bungalow longing for a shower and clean clothing. Perhaps a day of deep-sea fishing would clear his swollen head and cure him of his haunting dreams.

The men met in a darkened room in the rear of a New York dockside tavern where no one would care about their meeting or question their need for solitude.

"We have heard she's somewhere in one of the southern states." The first man's voice was harsh with a rough guttural accent.

The second man, his dark eyes cold as glass, stared at him. "Are you absolutely sure she is still alive? For all we know these reports about her could be a ploy to get us out in the open."

"There are papers about her. Very confidential papers that say there is a Mari Chandler who is not what she seems to be."

"Is the person who told you this someone you can trust?"

"Yes. He knows if he lies he will never see his family alive again."

"Then find out exactly where she is. My people will take it from there. If this woman is truly Alicia Brookes, she has information about our group we cannot allow to get out. For some reason she did not reveal this information when she was taken from our country. We know this because there were no reprisals for her imprisonment, but that does not mean she will not talk in the future. We have important people planted all over the world and we must make sure their identities are safe."

"When will I get paid for my information?"

"When you have accomplished the job." The second man didn't bother to tell him that payment would be in the form of a very cold and very sharp knife in the heart. The same kind of payment that was due Alicia Brookes, once she was found. She couldn't be allowed to divulge her knowledge of the network of terrorists scattered all over the world. He still didn't understand the reason for her silence over the years unless the report that stated that she had died as a result of injuries sustained during her imprisonment was true. This man was determined to find her no matter what it cost in money or manpower. To date, five men had died because they had given him false information. He did not suffer fools lightly. If this latest informant also lied, he would be taken care of without delay. If this new report was false, he would just continue his search, but if it was true he had to ensure that she would be terminated before something or someone forced her to talk.

CHAPTER TWO

Only by applying numerous coats of sunscreen was Mari able to escape a painful sunburn her first day on the beach.

She spent the morning exploring the hotel grounds and investigating the many nearby gift shops. After a light lunch of fruit salad and a glass of white wine, she bypassed the swimming pool in favor of spending the afternoon swimming in the ocean and lying on a chaise lounge nurturing her hope for a proper tan. Thanks to her efforts, by evening her skin was a pale gold.

For dinner, Mari donned a pale-lilac silk dress with spaghetti straps and a handkerchief hemline. She decided that she deserved special treatment for her first night in Mexico. She hadn't felt this elegant in a long time.

She felt a little uncomfortable eating alone in the large dining room, but that didn't stop her from enjoying the prawns and scallops she had ordered. After dinner, she wandered into the lounge since she didn't feel brave enough to venture down to the nearby village and visit one of the cantinas there without a male escort. She was able to secure a table far back enough from the dance floor to keep her from looking as if she wanted company but where she could still hear and enjoy the music. Unfortunately, it didn't deter the few more adventurous men who soon approached her.

Her coolly smiled refusal had worked until one man, who had obviously stayed too long at the bar, came up.

"Come on, baby, one dance won't hurt," he said in a slurred voice after hearing her refusal. He placed his palms in the middle of the small table and lurched forward.

Mari struggled not to choke on the whiskey fumes emanating from his swaying figure.

"I honestly don't care to dance," she said, her tone firmer and much colder than before.

"Hey, just one dance." He reached out to take her hand when another hand grabbed his wrist in an iron grip. The drunk looked up at the same time he felt a numbing sensation travel up his arm from a thumb pressed unobtrusively against a nerve.

"The lady doesn't care to dance," the stranger announced with a deadly calm. Recognizing authority, the drunk slunk away.

Mari looked up into a pair of eyes that glowed a deep, smoky gray in the dim light. Her mouth felt dry and her throat constricted. She felt as if she was standing in a never-ending tunnel as she was ensnared by his dark gaze. The room may have been warm but her blood still froze. Only by sheer force of will could she look at the man standing before her as if she didn't know him. Two inches over six feet tall, dark-auburn hair, gray eyes, and that same whiskey voice. Reid. She looked up at him praying her shock didn't show on her face. Judging from the faint smile on his lips, she looked calmer than she felt. He looked so good to her hungry eyes.

His pale-gold shirt was open at the collar and crisp navy dress slacks clothed a body used to much more casual attire. And his voice! The deep, raspy voice nudged memories that should have been forgotten a long time ago.

"Thank you for your assistance," she finally managed to say. She noticed his face looked wind-burned. Perhaps he had spent the day on one of the deep-sea fishing boats available to hotel guests.

That same distant smile appeared. "No problem. I'm just glad he was too drunk to want to start a battle." He sketched a salute and walked away.

Mari gulped down her margarita, not even tasting the tart mixture on her tongue. The man she had to cast out of her heart was there and he had barely looked at her!

Fool! her brain scolded. Did you expect him to recognize you? Besides, the new you isn't exactly his type, remember? He always liked skinny blondes. She looked down at her body, now curvier than usual courtesy of the ten extra pounds she had put on during her stay in the medical center. In keeping with her new identity, she didn't bother to diet them off. She watched Reid's figure amble between the tables until he stopped at one occupied by a Nordic-looking blond woman and took the opposite chair.

Naturally he would be with a blonde. Mari turned away and hastily gathered up her purse. She'd had more than enough of a fun evening. The idea that he might be here at *their* place with someone else burned like acid in her stomach.

She hurried to her bungalow and for the longest time sat in the dark looking out onto the beach. Only a few lovers walked along the water's edge.

She knew only one thing for certain. If Reid had brought someone else there, then it would be all that much easier to forget about him.

Mari should have known her sleep wouldn't be serene after the shock she'd already had. Except this dream wasn't dark and horrifying like before.

In the smoky mist of her dream, she wore a deep rose-pink nightgown of a sheer fabric that covered her body in a delicious haze. The style of nightgown Alicia had always preferred wearing.

Mari watched herself reclining on a bed covered with a burnt-orange fabric etched with an Aztec design. In the dream, her smile was filled with anticipation as she raised herself up on one elbow and beckoned to someone out of her view.

A man's broad back came into view and one tanned hand took her uplifted one to draw it to his lips. He joined her on the bed, his body half covering hers. The man was Reid!

From there, the vision bordered reality. It was as if Mari experienced the warm, comforting weight upon her. How good he felt against her!

His moist mouth leisurely explored every inch of her face and throat. His lips discovered unknown hollows in her cheeks and the dreamy upcurve of her mouth. His tongue penetrated her lips and beyond to thoroughly investigate each honeyed corner before rubbing against her tongue and drawing it into his mouth.

Mari moaned, moving restlessly under the sheet. It all seemed so real! She felt Reid's hand covering her breast, his thumb rotating her nipple into an aching nub through the cobwebby material. She put her arms around his back and lightly scored the breadth of solid skin with her nails.

"Please," she whispered. Her plea was answered as his hand moved slowly down to cup the juncture of her legs and press inward. The sheer material added an erotic caress to his intimate touch.

Mari gasped. Undaunted, she ran her hands over Reid's naked back and down to his tense buttocks. Each muscle was corded steel under her fingertips.

Her nightgown seemed to disappear and his hand was replaced by his lips on her breast. His tongue curled around her nipple and she wanted to scream with the pleasure he gave her.

Electric shocks raced through her body as his other hand continued to gently rub then lowered to probe with a touch that hinted of a much greater and more satisfying merging.

One hair-roughened leg slowly parted her thighs until his lower body rested heavily between them. His pulsing manhood teased the moist entrance with a few shallow thrusts while she arched upward in a silent plea for him to fully possess her. Her wish was finally granted when he entered her with the expertise of a man who knew his woman well.

Mari nipped his throat and heard his deep sensual groan. She arched up and dug her pink-tinted nails into his shoulders when he thrust into her with strong movements. Their rhythm was that of lovers who had known each other since the beginning of time.

The words he spoke against her neck were hot and erotic. He told her how much he enjoyed her passionate body and exactly what he would do to her next. Mari whimpered with happiness and replied with her own fantasies.

She moaned loudly, thrashing wildly among the rumpled bedcovers. Her lover increased his pace until they rose together to that cloud-covered peak. They were so close . . . so close . . . so . . .

"Augh!" Mari shot up in bed, her eyes wide open and her breathing erratic. She looked down, stunned to find her skin perspiring freely, her breasts swollen, the nipples taut, and the area between her thighs heavy with arousal. Her discarded nightshirt now lay on the floor. She couldn't even remember taking it off.

For one incredible moment, Mari was positive she had just made soul-shattering love with Reid. There was something too realistic about her fantasy encounter. The eerie chills started in her toes and worked their way up until she was shivering with a cold that had nothing to do with the temperature of the room. In fact, she had shut the air conditioning off and left the window open, so the room was very warm and humid. She looked toward the bathroom where the light had been left on and the door partially closed. By staring at the slim line of light she was able to feel a part of the present instead of the past.

She sensed that her dream was due to the shock of seeing Reid that evening and knowing that he was no longer hers. So her subconscious had given her a dream lover to replace the lost one.

"I can't take this!" She wailed to the silent spirits floating around her. "I cannot take this!"

At that same split second, Reid awoke with a vengeance. His breathing was ragged as if he had run a marathon and his body was slick with sweat. He felt the pain of an arousal from the incredibly erotic dream he'd just had.

It was a perfect reproduction of his and Alicia's last night there. She had worn a next-to-nothing pink nightgown and wasted no time in letting him know how much she wanted him. Their lovemaking had lasted all night, and each peak left them revived and wanting each other again.

He stumbled out of bed and into the bathroom for a cold shower. But even the cool water coursing over his shaking body couldn't dispel the chill in his heart and the heat in his lower abdomen. He was relieved that he hadn't taken Carole up on her invitation to join her in her room. He doubted that she would be very understanding that he had dreamed about another woman and then woken up more aroused than he had been in a long time. And anyway, he didn't think that Carole would be able to satisfy the hunger that had been three years in the making.

Just after he stepped out of the shower stall, Reid groaned and buried his face in his hands. Raw pain ripped through his body just as it had three years ago when he had learned that Alicia was dead. He wanted to let loose with an animal's cry of outrage at losing his mate. He had read that the wolf mated for life, and he understood the feeling well. Once a man finds the other half of his soul, how can he expect to find a replacement?

Mari decided decadence was wonderful with a capital W. She lay on the beach, soaking up the tropical sun and nursing a margarita. In fact, today she was having more fun people watching than soaking up the sun. If she wanted to admit the truth she was actually looking for one particular person, but a familiar dark auburn-haired man wasn't visible among the sunbathers.

She stretched her arms over her head. She was well aware that her blue-and-white striped bikini was sedate compared to the micro-bikinis worn by many of the other women, whether their figure was shapely or not. In deference to the heat she had pulled her hair up in a short perky ponytail and tied it with a blue ribbon.

"Señorita?"

She looked up, shielding her eyes from the bright sun with the back of her hand.

41

Oh, no. Mari sighed inwardly. He's looking for a rich American lady to pay his expenses.

The man was probably in his early twenties, simply dressed in a pair of clean white cotton shorts. His face and body could only be described as beautiful. By the white flash of his teeth as he smiled she could tell that he knew it too.

"I wondered if you would need a guide during your stay." He smiled again. "There are temple ruins not far from here and I can assist you in renting a car if you desire one and finding bargains in our marketplace."

With kickbacks from every merchant you guide me to, Mari thought to herself. She wasn't in the market for a guide or a lover. At least not him.

"Thank you, no," she said crisply, picking up her book to indicate that the conversation was over.

"But such a beautiful lady should not be alone," he protested, looking at her with limpid brown eyes.

"I like being alone."

"I am not expensive."

Mari was about to tell him off once and for all when another man's voice broke in.

"The lady said no thanks. So why don't you try your scam on someone else?"

Mari stiffened.

The young man looked at the intruder, saw the danger in his cold gray eyes, and escaped swiftly.

"It appears you're always rescuing me," Mari said lightly.

"It looked like you were handling him okay but these guys sometimes refuse to accept rejection,"

42

Reid told her with the same distant smile of the night before. "I'm just glad you were smart enough to recognize him for a con artist." He nodded his head and walked away.

Mari reached down for her book and found that her hands were shaking badly. How much more could she take? Especially when she saw Reid join the same blonde from the night before. She wanted nothing more than to run away but she forced herself to stay there for another hour. During that time she noticed the woman place her hand on his arm a few times but Reid never touched her. She wasn't sure whether to be relieved or unhappy.

Reid's afternoon was more productive. He returned to his bungalow two hours later to dress for his dinner date with Carole. Slender, blue eyes, and blonde. Just the way he liked them. So why didn't he feel more eager to spend the evening with such a lovely woman? Instead, the image of the curly-haired brunette in the blue-and-white bikini came to mind. She certainly wasn't his type. But there was something in her eyes when she looked at him. Those green eyes seemed to send him a message he couldn't read. It couldn't have been fear those two times he found men bothering her. She seemed composed enough and probably could have handled them on her own. He'd only stepped in because he figured an authoritative male figure wouldn't hurt.

As he stepped into the shower he found himself wondering why she was there alone. She wasn't beautiful—cute would be a better description for someone with such big eyes and a turned-up button nose. He ran the bar of soap over his chest. If he was smart he'd concentrate on Carole. Perhaps he was wrong to choose someone so much like Alicia, except that he felt better with someone who knew the score and Carole wasn't looking for more than a vacation fling with no strings attached.

Plus he was just a bit suspicious of how the woman seemed to need rescuing every time he was in the vicinity. It all could very well be an innocent coincidence, but he couldn't help wondering. After all, suspicion was his middle name. In his business he couldn't afford to trust anyone. He'd just have to see if she needed a knight in shining armor again and, if so, he'd make sure to stay very far away from her. On the other hand, he could also get closer to her and see what her game was. If she turned out to be from the other side, she'd soon learn that she wouldn't be able to seduce anything out of him. And if she turned out to be one of Lucas's personal spies, he'd make sure she took an earful back to her boss. Lucas was known to check on his people when they were on R and R, and that was one kind of spying Reid didn't appreciate.

After his shower, he walked back into the bedroom for clean underwear. As he glanced out a window, he noticed a familiar blue-and-white bikini hanging from the railing surrounding the tiny deck attached to the nearest bungalow. So the lady with the big green eyes and mysterious smile

44

was staying in bungalow 12. Maybe the question of what he would do had been taken out of his hands. His gut told him that there was a reason why she was staying there and he'd bet everything that it had to do with him. There could be no doubt now that he'd run into her again.

Mari enjoyed a leisurely bath before shampooing her hair and applying her makeup. She might be dining alone but that didn't mean she would stint on her appearance.

Tonight she wore a turquoise silk dress that had spaghetti straps to show off her new tan and a golden-yellow cobwebby belt to accent her slim waist. Her shoes and purse matched the belt. She curled her hair and brushed it out into soft waves feathering away from her face. When she looked into the mirror, she pronounced herself beautiful.

A half hour later, when Reid walked into the dining room with the stylishly dressed blonde on his arm, Mari didn't feel so beautiful. Actually, she was feeling downright ugly and very jealous! She had no appetite to finish her meal and left as soon as possible to return to her room and a not-so-hot book. But it was difficult to concentrate when visions of Reid making love to that blonde kept flashing before her eyes. The dream the previous night was the cause, she decided as she sighed and closed the book.

Mari turned out the lights and wandered out onto the deck. Her cotton nightshirt was cut on the brief side but the tiki torches lining the paths were too far away to reveal her scanty attire to any passerby. She hurt so much inside that she felt as if her entire body was tied up in knots. And it was all because of Reid. She wanted to find out his room number and march over there to tell him the entire incredible story.

There was the catch; it was so incredible she doubted he'd believe her. If it had been the other way around, she didn't think she'd believe anyone who would tell her the same story. Besides, she had given her word. No matter how much she disliked Lucas, she couldn't go back on it.

Oh, well. It had been her decision to come there and exorcise him from her soul. She allowed herself the fanciful thought that he just might be doing the same thing. She wanted to believe that even though Alicia had been dead for three years he couldn't forget her. Too bad she would never know the truth. To be on the safe side, she decided to stay out of Reid's way for the rest of her stay.

"Do you mind if I keep you company?" So much for resolutions made in the dead of night. Mari looked up from her breakfast to find Reid towering over her. Dressed in khaki shorts and a pale-blue polo shirt, he was enough to take her breath away. "By the way, I'm Reid Morgan."

"Please, sit down." She finally managed to get the words out. She gestured to the chair across from her. She wanted to ask him what had happened to the blonde, but then maybe she wasn't the type to get up before noon, and it was barely after eight in the morning. Or perhaps Reid had learned something about the woman he didn't like, such as that she worked for the other side, or even worse, for Lucas. Mari remembered a very suave diamond merchant in Amsterdam. He had plied Alicia with flowers and perfume and words of undying love while she learned he worked for a very unsavory group and turned the tables on him. The man was never seen nor heard of again. "I'm Mari Chandler," she said.

Reid glanced up when the waiter approached him and briskly ordered steak and eggs with blueberry muffins. He looked at Mari's meal of a poached egg and toast with a frown of disapproval. "That's barely enough to hold you for the next hour."

"It will definitely hold me. With the meals they feed you for lunch and dinner, not to mention the buffet set up by the pool, I have to cut calories whenever I can," she said lightly, sipping her coffee. She didn't really want any more but it gave her something to do. She set the cup down very carefully so as not to reveal that her hand was trembling.

Reid leaned back in his chair, his arm thrown loosely across the back. "Why would such a lovely lady come to a place like this alone?" He figured now was as good a time as any to begin his baiting and find out if she was something other than what she seemed.

Mari smiled. "Probably because I can be guaranteed time to myself. What about you? Do you get your kicks spying on couples? Or are you a reporter doing a story on romantic hideaways?"

Reid grinned. "Touché. No, I'm just an ordinary

working stiff looking for peace and quiet and some great deep-sea fishing."

Mari almost choked. An ordinary working stiff? That was the understatement of the year! The common working man didn't travel all over Europe eleven months out of the year. She wondered if he had a new partner and if that partner was female. But that was something else she wouldn't be finding out. In fact, if she was smart she would finish her breakfast in record time, make inane conversation for about three minutes, smile sweetly, and leave. Darn it, she swore she could smell the musky scent of his after-shave from across the table! How dare he still wear the same fragrance she had bought him for his birthday five years ago! How many other women had inhaled that scent while he possessed their bodies? She was better off not thinking about that either.

Meanwhile Reid was doing a little studying of his own. She might not be his type, but there was something about her that tugged at something deep inside of him that he thought had died a long time ago. Dressed in a red-and-white striped short jumpsuit with a broad red belt and her hair pulled up in a short ponytail, she could have been someone's kid sister, although he was positive she was over thirty. Yet there was something undefinable about her. Why did he feel that he had met her before? Or was this some kind of trick so he would drop his guard? No woman had ever broken behind his natural reserve, except one.

"I could use that old line about haven't I met

you someplace before but I don't think you would buy it," he mused with a bright sparkle in his eyes.

"You're right, I wouldn't," Mari murmured, looking down before he could read her fears in her face.

"So, why don't we exchange statistics?" he suggested.

"Such as?"

"I'm thirty-eight, in excellent health, born in Philadelphia, and I'm not married. So you see, I'm not just some sleeze on the make while the wife is off spending my money."

Mari couldn't help smiling at the way he rattled off statistics she already knew. "I'm thirty-two, my health is also excellent, and the proper term for my marital status is spinster."

Reid looked her up and down, at least what he could see above the table. "Spinsters are dried-up old prunes. No, I wouldn't classify you as one," he said huskily.

Mari's body melted. Between the look and voice she was rapidly turning into Jell-O. "What do you do for a living, Mr. Morgan?"

"I'm a construction engineer for an international firm," he said smoothly. "What about you?"

Mari hid her smile. The same answer he had been giving since Alicia first knew him. Some things never change. "I own a clothing boutique."

Reid dug into his breakfast with hearty gusto. He hadn't been this hungry in a long time. "Want a muffin?" he asked, holding out the basket filled with golden-brown blueberry muffins.

She shook her head. "My toast was just fine,

49

thank you. In fact, I should be going." She began to rise.

With the lightning speed Reid was famous for, he reached across the table and grasped her arm. "I'd appreciate the company," he told her in a low voice. "Please." He had to be careful around this lady. She made him feel things he didn't dare acknowledge.

His "please" was her undoing. She knew that wasn't a word normally in Reid's vocabulary, and she felt pleased that he wanted her company. She knew only too well if he didn't care he would have allowed her to go her merry way. In fact, he wouldn't have even bothered to sit down with her. Between his plea and his beseeching gaze she had no choice but to remain seated and sip another cup of coffee while Reid finished eating.

"Do you have any special plans for the day?" he asked casually, pushing his plate away.

Mari shrugged. "The usual high-energy activities. Lying by the pool or on the beach, go through the shops."

"Have you been in the village yet?"

She shook her head. "I've only been here a couple days, and in the beginning all I cared about doing was reminding my body it was all right to relax. My business keeps me very busy and I've been on a lot of buying trips lately."

"Would you care for an escort? I speak fluent Spanish," he offered, surprising himself. When he had woken up that morning he had thought about calling Carole and seeing if she would like to have a private picnic up the beach in a secluded cove

50

that he knew about. He knew she was definitely interested in him. She had invited him to her room again last night for a "nightcap," but he hadn't felt ready yet. Perhaps he should have taken her up on her offer. Then the memory of the explicit dream returned to him. No, he had been better off alone last night just in case the dream Alicia visited him once more. As it was, he hadn't fallen asleep until almost dawn and his sleep was fitful at best.

Mari hesitated. By all rights, she should discourage him. She should have told him she was married and waiting for her husband to join her or that she was a recent widow, but she knew he would have seen through her lies. Then something hardened inside. No, she wasn't going to give up this time with Reid. She would make sure he had no hint who she really was and she would take these limited hours with him and grab hold with both hands. Then she would have these memories to hold her for the lonely years ahead—because she now knew no man could ever take his place, no matter how hard she might try to find someone else to love.

"That sounds very nice, and I thank you for your offer as interpreter," she said demurely, deepening her drawl a bit more.

For one brief sizzling moment, Reid had the urge to discover the taste of her lips, which still held a trace of a deep-rose lip gloss. Before he could push the thought from his brain his body responded. What was it about this woman that attracted him on such an elemental level? She was turning out to be more dangerous than he first expected.

Luckily, Mari was unaware of his problem or she probably would have run for the hills. She merely smiled and requested ten minutes to freshen up. Reid managed an answering smile and nodded as Mari rose from the table and signed her check. He watched her leave through the arched doorway leading to the lobby. He remained seated, sipping his coffee. After talking with her and watching the way her eyes sometimes refused to meet his, he decided there was more to the lady than met the eye. He was determined to find out what it was.

Mari didn't really need to freshen up. But she did need some time alone to gather her thoughts together and wrap courage around her. She was a fool to go out with Reid, even for an innocent pastime like shopping, and when Lucas found out —and he certainly would learn about it from one of his personal spies—he would be furious. She doubted he would want the two of them to be in the same country, much less the same hotel!

Mari splashed cold water on her face and renewed her base makeup and blusher. She couldn't disguise the sparkle in her eyes at the thought of spending a few hours with Reid. It was all too good to be true. She grabbed her purse and fled her bungalow before she turned into the coward she felt like.

She found Reid in the lobby talking with the concierge about guided tours to the ruins near the resort and the various deep-sea fishing trips. She offered both men a friendly smile and accepted Reid's outstretched hand.

"Let's see how much money we can spend in a morning," he said, leading her out of the hotel. The village wasn't far away so they elected to walk since they could be back before the strong heat of the day descended on them.

"I hope the lady you were having dinner with last night won't object to my taking up your time this morning," Mari ventured.

"She's the kind of woman who will always land on her feet," he said carelessly, not daring to tell her that he'd already learned he preferred to be with her than with the always-smiling Carole with the scent of French perfume hanging heavily around her, her designer clothing, and her perfectly madeup face. For one wicked moment he wondered how she would handle it if she was marooned on a deserted island without her luggage and makeup case.

"Is it a joke you can share?" Mari asked, noticing the smile on his lips. Involuntarily, she recalled the many times she had kissed that smile into something much more intimate.

He chuckled. "I'm just picturing Carole on a deserted island *sans* luggage and makeup case, trying to open a coconut without breaking those claws she calls nails."

The blonde's name was Carole; it fit her. Mari couldn't help giggling at the picture Reid described.

Reid stopped short and swung around to face her. "How did those Southern gentlemen miss

53

you? And don't deny you're from the South because that slow drawl gave you away. By all rights you should be married and running after a couple of kids."

She lowered her head feeling the sting of tears in her eyes. Yes, by all rights she should have. Alicia and Reid had discussed having four children. "My fiancé was killed three years ago," she murmured. "It's only been recently that I've felt the need for company other than my own."

He swore under his breath. There was no disguising the pain she felt—pain he was only too familiar with. "I can truthfully say that I know what you're feeling. The woman I loved died about three years ago and she took a great part of my heart with her."

Mari bit her lip to keep from blurting out the truth. She knew she should turn around right now and run back to the hotel as if her life depended on it. How could she hope to keep her part of the bargain when the man she loved more than life itself hurt from the mistaken idea she was dead? But running away now would only arouse his suspicions. No, she would have to go through with her charade today, but she would make sure to stay out of his way and, if need be, would even leave the hotel to ensure that no other problems cropped up. She knew that if she saw him any more the temptation to tell him the truth would become too strong.

Sensing that he had upset her, Reid lightened his tone and suggested that they continue their walk. For the balance of the day, he was the most charming of companions. And Mari fell under his spell once again.

Reid translated sales pitches and advised Mari on the fine art of bargaining. She remembered how Alicia had been one of the last great bargainers when it came to looking for a good deal, but Mari was the kind of person to back down at the last minute. There wasn't a reckless bone in her body. Reid wasn't about to allow her to do that, and many times he urged her to walk away until the craftsman moaned how the lovely señorita was causing him to lose much money, and how would he be able to feed his many children, even as he lowered his price. In the end, Mari was the proud owner of several lovely pieces of hammered silver jewelry and colorful woven baskets.

Around noontime, when the sun was overhead and merciless, Reid suggested they return to the hotel to eat. While the local food was probably excellent, it could also leave innocent stomachs with a good case of *turista*. Mari wanted to make an excuse not to eat with him but couldn't think of a plausible one, so she allowed him to lead her back to the hotel and outside to the veranda where light lunches were served. When Reid next suggested a swim, she agreed and also agreed to have dinner with him that evening. She did beg off when he wanted to go dancing. By then her nerves were at a breaking point and she badly needed time to herself. And when he asked if she would like to meet for breakfast the next morning, she mumbled an excuse and escaped before he could pin her down.

Mari hadn't been in her bungalow for more than ten minutes when the telephone rang.

"Yes." Her voice was crisp and cool.

"You're playing with fire, Mari. I don't like that." Lucas was more than a little intimidating, but then that was his way of keeping his people in line. Too bad he refused to remember that she wasn't one of his people any longer.

"I haven't given him any hint as to who I am and I don't intend to." Her resolution not to see Reid again went by the wayside as soon as she heard Lucas's voice.

"Check out of there first thing in the morning. I'll arrange a room for you in Acapulco or wherever you want to go. We'll take care of all your expenses."

"No."

The silence on the other end was deafening.

"Just remember that your stupidity could cause his death. They're still looking for Alicia. They don't believe she's dead."

Mari swallowed, her eyes closed against the horror of Reid's splendid body lying in a broken heap in a dark alley.

"I've followed your orders for many years now, but I don't have to answer to you any longer. If rumors are hot and heavy, you should be able to quash them. You're certainly good at doing it when it suits your purpose. I don't intend to give myself away and I will not allow you to take this time away from me," she said coldly, mustering up all the courage Alicia was known for. "At the end of two weeks I will be flying back to North Caro-

56

lina and he will be none the wiser. In fact, I haven't even told him exactly where I'm from and I will not drop even a hint. In return, you will leave us alone and recall your spy from down here. You owe me, Lucas." She thought of a bungled operation in the Middle East where she had ended up the victim and knew her former superior would recall the same incident.

"If you screw this up you'll wish you had died in that prison." The call clicked off before she could reply.

Mari slowly replaced the phone, noticing how badly her hand was shaking. She wouldn't be surprised if Reid received a call from Lucas recalling him to Washington, D.C. Perhaps that was for the best. She curled up on the bed, gathering the covers over her to ward off the chill that was beginning in her heart and moving upward to overtake her entire body. Morning was a long way off.

CHAPTER THREE

Reid wasn't in the best of moods the next day.

First, Mari had run off last night for no reason at all, then he had received a call from Lucas demanding that he return immediately to D.C. and refusing to give a reason. Reid had told him in succinct terms what he could do with his demand and had hung up on him. He knew his refusal wouldn't deter Lucas for long, but it might buy him some much-needed time to find out what had upset Mari. A part of him still felt she wasn't what she claimed to be, but he was beginning to wonder if he was just being overly suspicious.

He hadn't slept well, which only decreased any goodwill he might have had to begin with.

After a quick shower he dressed in a yellow T-shirt and navy shorts and sought Mari out in the dining room. When he couldn't find her he called her bungalow and even pounded on her door. He then had her paged throughout the hotel and next searched the pool area, the beach, and the tennis courts. Beginning to panic, something Reid wasn't known to do, he checked the village. Since there were no guided tours leaving that morning, he knew there were few places she could be. But Reid wasn't about to give up. He'd find her if it killed both of them!

Mari had found the small inlet by instinct alone. She remembered how Alicia and Reid had spent many private hours there. A natural waterfall spilled down from a pile of rocks about eight feet above the ground into a small pool of water below. With the greenery surrounding the pool and the empty sandy beach leading to the ocean, she felt assured of privacy.

After her talk with Lucas the previous night Mari had spent several hours alternating between tears and rage toward the man who thought he could run her life when he had no right to. By morning she was still upset and unable to even think of eating breakfast. Instead, she walked down the beach to the tiny cove.

She sat cross-legged on the sand tossing tiny pebbles into the water and vacillating between staying there where she could see Reid or taking Lucas up on his offer for an all-expense-paid vacation in Acapulco.

When Reid stumbled onto Mari an hour later, he didn't know whether to shake her senseless for scaring him by disappearing like that or pull her into his arms and never let her go. How had she found this place? The many times he and Alicia had come there they were never disturbed. It should have upset him that Mari had invaded a place that was so special to him, but for some strange reason she seemed right sitting by the pool and looking into the water. The conflicting emotions left him feeling angry and frustrated at himself. Sure, he'd come down to Mexico to let Alicia go, but he didn't expect this wide-eyed brunette to accomplish the job for him. What was so special about her? Why did she make him feel things he thought long dead?

"Who're you hiding from—me?" he asked in a rough voice.

Mari's head snapped up. Whatever anger Reid had felt evaporated at the sight of her reddened eyes and puffy face. She hastily swiped the back of her hand across damp cheeks. She didn't want to see him just yet. Not until she got her thoughts straightened out. Why couldn't he just disappear for a while?

"If you don't mind I'm not really in the mood for company right now," she murmured, looking down into the pool of water as if she'd find all her answers there.

Reid remained standing off to one side, noticing her simple white cotton crop top with a U-shaped neckline that bared her collarbones and pale-blue shorts with an elasticized waistband. Alicia's choice of outfit would have been more daring, something brief and colorful to tease his senses. Looking at Mari's bent head, he wanted nothing more than to stride over there and pick her up and make love to her on the sand. The force of such an erotic thought left him shaken.

Mari was aware that he was still there and wished he'd leave, but she knew he wouldn't. Reid had questions to ask and he wasn't about to leave until they were answered.

"May I sit down?" Reid asked formally. Receiving no reply, he walked over to a spot to Mari's left and sat down. "And how are you feeling this beautiful morning? Did you sleep well?" He'd hazard a guess her slumber had been as ravaged as his own.

She looked at him out of the corner of her eye. "Why are you here?"

For once Reid had no glib answer. "I don't know, but I had to find you and make sure you were all right."

"You're better off with Carole, Reid," she said softly, looking down at her hands lying in her lap. The hours between midnight and dawn had been agonizing. She knew being with Reid was hazardous, but she didn't want to give in to Lucas's demands either. In the end she felt so confused she knew she had to go away to someplace quiet where she wouldn't be disturbed. The place where Alicia and Reid had spent so many pleasurable hours was where she ended up. The trouble was, it only caused memories to surface that were better off left buried. And seeing the cause of all her troubles appear didn't make her feel any better.

"I a very good guide, señorita," Reid said in an exaggerated Spanish accent. "I show you ruins, help you buy pretty things. I a good guide, señorita."

Mari's giggle turned into a hiccup. It was enough to break the tension flowing between

61

them. "That is the worst German accent I have ever heard."

"That was Spanish!"

"Could have fooled me."

Reid cupped Mari's chin with caressing fingertips and turned her face toward him.

"Don't cry," he whispered, his mouth moving closer. "I'm a helpless dolt around crying women."

Her breath caught in her throat. "I can't imagine you ever feeling helpless," she whispered, her lips parted for his kiss. But Reid had other plans.

"With you I am."

His mouth found the damp salty tracks on her cheeks and carefully licked them away. Each eye was soothed by the healing touch of his tongue lapping up any future tears. A soft sigh escaped Mari's lips when Reid shifted closer to take advantage of her moist open mouth.

The kiss that should have started out gentle quickly escalated into a fierce hunger rarely experienced between two strangers. Of course, they weren't really strangers.

Shaken by the earthquake rolling in the middle of his body, Reid broke away for a second, looked down into Mari's glazed eyes, then returned to the lush garden of delights her mouth offered. His tongue penetrated her mouth with ease, setting up an age-old rhythm. Her breast heaved under his exploring hand as he drew her lower lip into his mouth and nibbled. He heard her throaty moans, felt her nipple contract to a hard nub under his fingers, and inhaled the womanly fragrance of her skin. For a long while he was catapulted back in time as the world shifted around him. He stretched out, pulling her over him at the same time that his hands tunneled under her crop top to roam over her back and around to bare breasts. The juncture of her thighs fit snugly against him. He felt her hand move slowly under his shirt and along the waistband of his shorts.

Reid's eyes were closed but all his other senses were working overtime as he felt the soft body melt over him. She fit perfectly with him and he could easily visualize a more intimate fitting of their bodies.

"Alicia, I love you so much." He groaned, burying his face against sweet-smelling skin.

The world suddenly ground to a bone-jarring halt. He opened his eyes and saw a red-faced Mari refuse to look at him as she scrambled to her feet and straightened her clothing.

"Mari, I am so sorry." He sighed, raking his hair back with shaking hands. He swore under his breath.

She shook her head. Right now she was too full of painful anger to speak coherently. She moved away a few feet before she gave in to her first instinct and bashed his face in.

"No wonder you're no longer with Carole." She choked. "You can't even remember what woman you're with."

"*Mari!*" Reid's shout was ignored as she ran along the sand toward the hotel. He pounded his fist into his open palm. "Damn, damn, damn!" How could he have done anything so stupid? Over the past three years he'd had a very few fleeting affairs that were nothing more than physical release. Then he meets a woman who's warm and funny and he screws it up the minute he reaches first base! He'd have to do a great deal of groveling to get back into Mari's good graces.

Then it hit him. Those one-night stands used to leave him angry at himself for feeling guilty and empty in spirit. This time there was no guilt, only sorrow that he had hurt Mari. He realized that it was being in the cove that had brought Alicia's name to his lips. The pain of her death had finally left him, thanks to Mari. He only hoped she would eventually forgive him.

Mari returned to her bungalow and indulged herself in an old-fashioned temper tantrum. She tossed pillows across the room, flung her clothing to the floor, and ripped all the magazines to shreds.

"He's kissing *me* and saying he loves *her!*" She shrieked, stamping into the bathroom and turning on the shower. "I'm my own rival!" She threw off her clothes and stood under the cool water in an attempt to diffuse her anger. She was so furious she wouldn't have been surprised if clouds of steam had risen up around her. Suddenly her temper dissipated. She had never felt more like crying and she decided that there was no better time to break down in a real crying jag than now.

Reid felt very confused. What was it about Mari that called out to him so strongly? She was nothing at all like the women in his past. Still . . . he settled back on the bed, his hands clasped behind his head. Kissing her felt familiar, as did holding her in his arms. Then he messed everything up by recalling someone else. No, not just someone else, someone who had been a very important part of his life.

He sighed as he turned over to grab the phone. It was time to make amends. Hopefully she would listen to him.

Mari had few weaknesses—flowers was one of them. Especially yellow roses from Reid with the request they meet for drinks. She kept standing before the vase to inhale the heady fragrance. How could she continue feeling angry at him when the woman he'd actually called out to was *her?* Was it something to do with the way she kissed? Was a woman's kiss like fingerprints—were no two alike?

She knew she was wishing for the impossible. She wanted to feel the hard strength of his body against hers, hear his sensual murmurs, see his glazed eyes when he reached that peak with her. She was selfish, she wanted it all. She may not be Reid's type of woman now but he was still physically attracted to her, whether he wanted to be or not, and she'd do everything possible to experience his lovemaking again. Even if it meant selling her soul.

Her lips curved in a wry smile. Now, that sounded like something Lucas would suggest. She had always thought of him as a spawn of the devil.

Mari knew she was treading on dangerous

ground. Alicia had thrived on danger the way an alcoholic lived for a drink. She had never taken unnecessary chances but she had enjoyed the flow of adrenaline in her system as she worked in enemy territory. She used to claim it made life more exciting.

Mari's idea of taking a chance was buying the generic brand of aluminum foil. She wanted her life nice and steady and, most especially, safe. Danger wasn't a part of Mari Chandler's life.

And here she had thought she could cut Alicia and Reid out of her life. She'd had no idea Reid would reappear and that her insatiable hunger for the man would only increase.

Mari kept expecting to hear from Lucas again. Surely he wasn't going to back down after their one confrontation? She was certain he had been surprised by her stubborn refusal to give in. He wouldn't know love if it hit him square in the face.

She dressed in cream-color pleated cotton trousers and a softly styled apricot blouse. She pinned one of the roses to her collar before she left her bungalow and headed for the outdoor bar where Reid had said he would be waiting for her. Seeing Reid sitting at a corner table, she stopped at the entrance. Watching him sit alone, a fierce wave of longing and hunger swept over her. She wanted nothing more than to tell him the truth. She wanted to see his eyes darken with love the way they did years ago. She wanted to hear the words again. But that wasn't to be. And she would be better off if she remembered that. She noticed that the glass in front of him was half empty and he looked tense. Was he afraid she wouldn't show up? Deciding it was time to put him out of his misery, she walked swiftly toward his table.

Reid had just about decided that Mari hadn't forgiven him after all when he saw her heading toward him. He noticed she wore one of his roses and felt hope warming his insides. His first reaction was to rush forward and take her into his arms and steal her away to his bungalow. Luckily, he stayed those impulses and settled for lurching to his feet.

"I'm sorry I'm late," Mari murmured, flashing a smile that sent heat waves throughout his body.

"I—" He swallowed. "I figured you weren't coming, and I wouldn't have blamed you." He assisted her into the chair next to his and looked up with an irritated glance when a waitress approached them. Mari ordered a margarita and Reid asked for another scotch.

Mari remained silent until the waitress returned with their drinks.

"Reid, I would prefer we forget about some things," she said quietly, sipping her drink.

He exhaled a sigh of relief. He hadn't expected to be let off the hook that easily. He was surprised that Mari could be so understanding.

"Alicia was someone you loved a great deal, wasn't she?"

Reid nodded. Perhaps this was the time to start talking about her. "We used to work together," he explained. "The usual story: We fell in love, wanted to get married. But something happened and she was killed."

His words were stripped bare of feelings, but Mari saw the stark horror in his eyes. He still hadn't gotten over Alicia.

"We—ah—we came here not long before she was killed," he went on, fiddling with his glass. "In fact, I proposed to her during our stay. In that cove."

Mari felt sick to her stomach. How could she sit there and look carefully noncommittal when he was talking about her?

"How long ago did it happen?" She sipped her drink in an effort to look calm.

"Three years. I came back in order to set her spirit free." He slowly raised his eyes to her pale features. "You're the first woman who's allowed me to forget her."

That was when Mari knew she shouldn't have met Reid that night. This wasn't at all what she expected. He had been going through the same kind of pain that she had during the past three years. She cursed Lucas for doing this to them and cursed herself for allowing him to bully her.

"Letting go of the past is very difficult to do," she murmured. "Books say it's important to look to the future but I sometimes wonder if the future will be any better."

Reid sensed it again—the tingling sensation that she was not what she claimed she was. Was she from the other side, looking to trip him up or find something to blackmail him with? It had happened in the past. In fact, a very lovely scientist had once tried her lovely wiles on him only to be circumvented by a very jealous Alicia.

68

"Reid, I learned a long time ago that it's best to keep on going forward. If you don't you tend to backslide into a world that is no longer real," Mari said softly, breaking into his thoughts. This was so much more difficult than she had expected. She knew she was lying to him and he would never have the chance to learn the truth. She felt so torn up inside! "Hey." She injected a soft laugh. "If we sit around here too long we're going to end up two very sad drunks, and I'm not very good with alcohol on an empty stomach."

Reid looked up and flashed that heart-stopping grin. "Does this mean you're willing to have dinner with me too?"

"Must be since I'm not going to allow you to get me drunk," she retorted lightly, finishing her margarita. "I haven't eaten since breakfast and I happen to be starving for the works—enchiladas, carnitas, tacos, burritos, you name it."

He raised an eyebrow. "And another margarita?"

She wrinkled her nose. "That too."

They kept their lighthearted manner during dinner, and this time Reid was able to persuade Mari to accompany him into the lounge for dancing.

Mari was in seventh heaven. Now she didn't have to worry about drunken men approaching her. Only one thoughtless gentleman had come up to their table to ask her to dance, but one look at the dark expression on Reid's face was enough to send him slinking back to his table.

"You're scaring off my future suitors," she

chided as they moved across the dance floor as one. She had forgotten how wonderful it was to have his arms around her and how well he and Alicia danced together.

"Good," he grumbled, surprised at how well they danced together. Only one other woman had ever picked up his signals as fast as Mari did. It was almost uncanny.

Mari couldn't remember a more perfect evening. Her drink was more melted ice than alcohol since she and Reid spent most of their time on the dance floor. She vowed no one would interfere with the time she and Reid had together, not even Lucas. And she meant to keep that vow. There would be time enough for self-recrimination when she returned to Charlotte.

After the lounge closed they walked down to the beach where they slipped off their shoes and rolled up their pant legs in order to walk in the surf.

"The sky is so clear here," Mari commented, tipping her head back to look up at the black sky. "If I was the corny type I'd say it looked like black velvet with diamonds sparkling against it."

Reid looked down at her face, washed with moonlight. "You're the one who's sparkling."

She tilted her head to one side. "Why, sir, you say the nicest things." If she had been a cat she would have been purring.

He stopped, grabbed hold of her hand, and raised it to his lips. "I only say the truth, Mari." He emphasized her name. He wanted to make damn sure she knew he was aware whom he was with.

Nibbling on her fingertips as if they were dessert, he drew her forefinger into the heated moisture of his mouth as he gazed down into her eyes, which gleamed like bright emeralds in the silver light overhead. He wished he could understand the expression in the green depths. He sensed that she was trying to hide something from him. Was she afraid he'd say the wrong name again? But he doubted he would make that mistake a second time. Mari was rapidly becoming a part of him. He wanted to make love to her, needed to, but he sensed that that would have to wait. Something, or someone, had hurt her and he was determined to take it nice and slow until she was ready for him. Reid wondered if an hour would be long enough.

Mari's tongue swept over her lips. "I'm not very good at holiday affairs, Reid," she murmured, using her other hand to comb the dark silky strands away from his forehead. "I'm not the kind of woman to take a vacation and lover at the same time and blithely leave with just memories and souvenirs of a two-week getaway."

Reid tensed. "Is there someone else?" he asked hoarsely.

She shook her head, thinking of the few men she had gone out with and how none of them meant anything to her. "I'm just trying to say that my emotional makeup doesn't allow me to go to bed with one man one night and look around for someone new the next day after breakfast. If you're looking for a quick affair I suggest you try someone else. I'd only be a lost cause."

He smiled and shook his head. "No, I can never

71

see you as a lost cause. Choosy, yes, and that's good. I don't go to bed with every woman I meet because I'm just as particular. Yes, I'd like to make love to you. I'd be a fool if I said differently, but give me the credit to take it as slow as possible." So much for his one-hour time limit. "There's no reason why we can't be friends, is there? I promised you excellent guide service to the ruins and that you shall get." He kissed each knuckle on her hand. "Besides, haven't you ever heard that rushing into something takes all the fun out of it? Without anticipation, there's no joy."

Of course I've heard that, she wanted to scream. Alicia said it! She told you that when you sat in the little café in Budapest before you returned to that tacky little hotel to make love. She lowered her eyes to hide the agitation in the emerald depths.

Assuming her silence meant agreement, Reid wrapped his arm around her shoulders and guided her up the sand toward the bungalows. "And if we're going to play tourist tomorrow you better get some sleep."

Mari pulled away. "How did you know where I was staying?" she asked suspiciously.

"A very distinctive blue-and-white bikini hanging from the deck railing," he replied. "I happen to be in the next bungalow."

Mari bit back her gasp. She had felt safe as long as she thought Reid was staying in the hotel proper, but to find out he was so close was enough to raise her temperature.

"Look at it this way. I'm close by if you have a nightmare or something," he told her, keeping

72

her close to his side as they approached her bungalow.

Mari thought about one particular dream. It was
listed more under "or something" than a nightmare.

When they reached her door, Reid moved in
until Mari's back was pressed against the wood.
His hands rested just above her shoulders, captur-
ing her within his loose embrace.

"I said I wouldn't hurry you about making love,"
he murmured. "I didn't say I wouldn't kiss you
good night."

"That's a relief," she couldn't resist saying.

This kiss was gentle. Reid's lips coasted over
hers time and time again until she hungered for
the hard pressure. Mari slipped her arms around
his waist and drew him closer until their bodies
rested against each other. A daring flick of her
tongue rediscovered his musky taste and a soft
sigh of satisfaction escaped her lips.

The need for gentleness was suddenly gone.
Reid gathered her fully into his arms and his
mouth slanted over hers with a hunger that was as
strong as her own. His mouth possessed her the
way his body wished to. The warm scent of his
after-shave mingled with the sweet floral of her
perfume to make the most potent of aphrodisiacs.
Mari dug her fingers into the strong-muscled back,
massaged the tension away, and slipped them upward to find his vulnerable nape and silky hair.

Their bodies melted together, and they were
both filled with wonder that a simple kiss could

escalate into something so beautiful. Mari shifted her body, wanting to be as close to him as possible.

Reid felt the same, wishing he could crawl inside of her body and stay there for the rest of his life.

"I want to be inside you," he whispered roughly. "I want to take you to bed and make love to you until you're aware there is no one but me."

"There is no one but you."

He exhaled a heavy breath. Her honesty could very well be their undoing if he didn't exercise some control. He had promised her time and here he was talking about taking her to bed. All right, he would keep that promise, but that didn't mean he had to leave her right away. He rested his forehead against hers.

"You make it very difficult for me to keep my word about not rushing you," he confessed. "And, Mari, no matter how much I ache tonight I do intend to keep it."

She looked up with her big green eyes glistening in the moonlight. "Even if you leave me aching too?"

He laughed harshly. "Oh, lady, you really know where to hit a guy. As much as I hate to say it, yes, I am going to take myself off to my solitary bed and tomorrow we'll do some sightseeing. When I do make love to you I want to make sure there won't be any regrets on either side." He dropped a lingering kiss on her forehead, slowly disengaged his arms, and walked away without looking back.

Mari remained in the same spot until Reid disappeared from view. Moving slowly, she entered her room and headed for the bathroom. She withdrew a small leather case from her cosmetic bag and took out a plastic vial. Then she leaned over the sink, opened one eye very wide, and blinked. A green disk dropped into her open palm and she dropped it into one half of the vial. A matching disk was placed in the other side. When she looked at a woman she didn't completely recognize in the mirror, she saw a face flushed from Reid's kisses and lips swollen and a bright pink. But the main difference was the dark blue-purple eyes that stared back at her. Alicia's eyes in Mari's face.

Taking a deep breath, Mari stilled her trembling hands and set about to clean her lenses. She would leave them out tonight and put them back in tomorrow morning. She cleansed her face, took a quick shower, and slipped on a nightgown before crawling into bed. She knew if nothing else happened she would still have Reid's kisses to remember, and they could be just as potent as his love-making. When she finally did fall asleep a smile was on her lips.

"Okay, lady, rise and shine!" A pounding on her door preceded the familiar voice.

Mari half rose up, her eyes squinting to shut out the early morning light. "Reid?" she questioned in a voice husky with sleep.

"You got it. Now let me in," he ordered in a jovial voice.

Her face lit up. Mari was out of bed in a flash and had her hand on the doorknob when she remembered something.

"Ah, just a second," she called out, racing for the bathroom.

"Mari, are you all right?" Reid demanded from the other side of the door after a couple minutes passed. "If you don't let me in soon I'm going to pick this sorry excuse for a lock!"

"Reid, please, just give me a minute," she pleaded, inserting the lenses and taking the time to quickly brush her teeth. Early-morning bad breath wasn't her idea of greeting a good-looking man.

When she did open the door, Reid swept her into his arms and placed a hearty kiss on her lips. "Um, the lady took the time to brush her teeth," he murmured, nuzzling her neck. "And added a bit of perfume." He began to leisurely explore her mouth until she was left breathless. "You not only taste sexy but smell just as good. What more can a man want—unless it's to wake up next to that particular lady."

Mari laughed. "Reid, you're incorrigible." She kept her arms looped around his neck. If she had her way she wouldn't move one inch.

He looked down at her face, bright with a smile, eyes sparkling, and wondered how he deserved someone as warm as her. Whatever it was, he wasn't going to look a gift horse in the mouth.

"You're giving me ideas again," he warned, the husky note in his voice and tension in his body telling her exactly what those ideas were.

Mari dropped her arms and stepped away once

his own arms left their comfortable position around her waist.

"If you intend to act like a gentleman perhaps you should tell me why you woke me up at the crack of dawn," she suggested, wanting nothing more than to draw him into her bed for a morning romp.

Reid looked her over, sleep-tousled hair, features flushed from a combination of just waking up and his kisses, and pouting lips. She was such a temptation!

"If you brought any with you, put on some grubby clothes," he told her, eyeing the cobalt silk nightgown with male appreciation.

"Grubby clothes and an exclusive vacation resort don't go together."

"Maybe not, but deep-sea fishing and fancy duds don't either."

Mari quickly hid her dismay. There were few bits of Alicia's personality that Mari kept, and an abhorrence of deep-sea fishing—in fact, fishing of any kind—was one of them.

"Sounds like fun." She didn't sound excited. "I'll —ah—I'll see what I can find." She moved away to rummage in the drawers and pulled out a pair of cutoffs and a T-shirt before escaping into the bathroom.

Reid moved around the bungalow rubbing his hands together with glee. One of his favorite sports was deep-sea fishing and he was looking forward to sharing the day with Mari. He sensed they were going to have a great day together.

Ironically, he was so caught up in his dream of a perfect day that he forgot he was standing in the bungalow that he and Alicia had shared a few years ago. He was beginning to heal.

CHAPTER FOUR

To Mari's way of thinking it wasn't the great day Reid had promised her. Her nose was sunburned, her skin was dried out from the stiff ocean breeze, her stomach was uneasy from the pitch and roll of the fishing boat, and her face was frozen from the eternal smile she flashed at Reid as he excitedly showed her how to cast out and reel in the fishing line that she really didn't care to hold onto. Alicia had always remained on the dock waving Reid off for his day of fun on the ocean and gaily wishing him luck while she spent her hours by the swimming pool. If Mari never stepped on board another fishing boat for the rest of her life, it would be too soon.

She also couldn't understand why beer had to be consumed in such great quantities. Luckily, there were a few cans of diet cola available, and she was grateful for them since she had never been very fond of beer and her uneasy stomach demanded something fizzy to calm it down.

"This is the life," Reid said with a contented sigh, leaning back in the chair, the seat belt around his waist loosening with his motion. "Just man against nature. If I can catch a marlin today I'll be in hog heaven."

"Sounds great." Mari just barely managed a proper smile. *Wasn't it time to head back to the marina?* Her hair was so sticky from the salt spray she doubted she would ever be able to wash it out. She was praying that Reid would soon suggest returning when a healthy tug on his line caught his attention.

"Hot damn!" he shouted, sparing the skipper a brief glance. "Manuel, I'd say we've got a big one here."

"*Sí*, Señor Reid." The dark-skinned man grinned, walking to the stern of the boat. "Play with him the way you play with a beautiful woman." He smiled at Mari who was silently cursing the rude fish for lengthening her day. She slid her sunglasses on and watched Reid play with the fish in a dance of wills. She had no doubt that Reid would win in this elemental battle.

Something primitive happened while Mari watched Reid work with the large fish. She couldn't help noticing the deep tan the day's sun had intensified, the play of sleek muscles as he worked with the fishing rod, the sheen of his skin from perspiration rolling down his arms and chest. The temperature around her rose by about fifty degrees and she felt her mouth drying. Dressed in cutoffs that were damp with sea water and molded to his muscular thighs and a pair of beat-up deck shoes, Reid looked more male than she felt she could handle at that moment. Mari was remembering the nights Reid's dark skin had been damp from another sort of exertion—when he would look down at Alicia with those beautiful eyes, dark with passion, and his mouth curved in a smile guaranteed to make her want him again and again. Mari couldn't keep her eyes from him. They wandered over his shoulders and arms straining with the effort to keep the fish's head up, his broad chest glistening with sweat from his efforts, and his thighs taut with strain. Mari thought of many hot afternoons where Reid's energy had been expended in a more pleasurable way.

Soon, along with Mari's physical awareness of Reid, came her interest in his skill in handling the fish.

"Don't lose him!" she screamed suddenly, standing up and running over to his side.

"Honey, I don't intend to," Reid informed her between clenched teeth. The muscles in his arms were screaming with pain but he wasn't about to let up now. He was certain this was the largest marlin he had ever landed, and he wasn't going to give up his trophy after the long hard fight he had put up.

The hours passed as Mari watched Reid, with Manuel's help, end the battle.

"He is huge, Señor Reid," the skipper told him with a broad grin. "No one has caught a fish this big in a long time. You should be proud." He held up a rifle.

"A dream come true," Reid breathed.

Mari's eyes widened at the sight of the rifle. "You're not going to shoot him, are you?" Her voice rose with indignation.

"Mari, this isn't like trout fishing. These guys don't tire as easily and the only way we're going to be able to get him into the boat is to shoot him." Reid kept his attention on the thrashing fish. "Don't worry, Manuel is an excellent shot. The marlin won't feel a thing."

Mari whipped off her sunglasses and grabbed his arm. "But it doesn't seem fair," she protested. "After all, he doesn't have anything to fight back with but his strength. And who says he doesn't feel anything? Doctors love that phrase, but I always felt what they claimed I wouldn't feel."

Reid looked down at widened green eyes silently imploring him to have pity. He uttered a pungent curse under his breath. Deep-sea fishing was his love and a sport he rarely had time for. He hadn't caught a fish this large before; this marlin was his lifelong dream, but he knew he would set it free. And all because a lovely woman with large green eyes asked him to.

"Oh, hell." He sighed, freeing the line enough for the fish to go free.

"Señor!" Manuel cried out.

Reid continued looking into Mari's face, seeing her distress dissolve into happiness. "Mari, I'm beginning to think you're going to prove to be a lot of trouble to me."

Her smile was pure sunshine. "Then I'll just have to make it up to you." There wasn't a trace of coyness in her voice.

"Yeah, I think so." His own voice was husky with the same innuendo.

The ride back to the marina was silent. Manuel

was unhappy over losing a fish he could have bragged about to the other ship captains over a beer in the tavern. Reid wondered how he could have given up the fish of a lifetime just because a woman asked him to. And Mari wondered if she had gone too far in asking him to let the fish go. The payment he might ask in return could be much more than she dare give him.

When they reached the marina, Mari begged off having a drink with Reid, explaining that she wanted to do nothing more than stand under a hot shower. He was tempted to ask if there was room for one more but decided this wasn't the time to push it since she seemed so skittish. In order to give Mari plenty of time to shower and relax, he suggested meeting for dinner in two hours.

"That sounds wonderful," she agreed, pretending not to notice the hot expression in his eyes. She had to remember her promise to Lucas and not give in to Reid's very potent charm. Why did she have to come on so strong to him on the boat? Ever since she had first seen and talked to him, she had handled this all wrong. "I'll meet you at the restaurant?"

He was surprised by her suggestion since they were virtually neighbors but sensed that she had a reason for suddenly putting distance between them, and decided to honor her request. "That's fine," he said. After speaking with Manuel and planning another day of fishing, he escorted Mari back to her bungalow.

Reid entered his own bungalow and stripped off his sweaty clothing, planning on a long cool shower. He smiled when he recalled Manuel leaning forward and whispering, "Señor, perhaps the lovely lady would prefer to remain behind next time since she doesn't seem to enjoy fishing." Reid had chuckled. He had to agree that it might be a better idea. If that marlin decided to grab hold of his hook again, nothing and, hopefully, no one was going to free it.

He frowned as he remembered Mari's sudden switch in personality. For a moment there on the boat he was positive she was silently suggesting they adjourn to her room for a little relaxation when they got back. Could she be from the other side after all? Was she there to seduce him, maybe tempt him to change sides? No, if anyone with an ounce of smarts wanted him they would follow his tastes in women to the letter. They would ensure he'd meet up with a nice slim blonde who was dynamite in bed and had a mind of her own. Someone like Carole or . . . No, some thoughts were better off not aired. If Carole had been sent there to do a job on him, she certainly hadn't tried very hard. The last time he had seen her she had been on the arm of a wealthy-looking Latin man. Funny, she was the kind of woman he normally would have gone for, and ended up having a great time, in bed and out. But this time he found something missing. Strangely, that missing link was found in, of all people, Mari Chandler. A cute brunette with her snub nose and fragile ways caught his attention in the way only one other woman had ever been able to. He wasn't interested in a long-term relationship because he knew he could never find another Alicia. One true love was all he would be allowed to have in this lifetime, he knew. Still, he couldn't resist wondering what Mari would be like in bed. Would she be a sweet purring kitten or a clawing wildcat? Perhaps a bit of both? It would certainly be interesting to find out. He stepped into the shower and picked up the bar of soap, and ran it over his chest. He'd always believed in positive thinking, and thinking about Mari in his bed was about as positive as he could get.

Mari was relaxing in a warm tub of bubble-topped water and thinking about Reid just as strongly as he was thinking about her. Except she already knew what kind of lover he was, and her body was aching for his special touch. How many times had he literally made her body sing? He always knew what pleased her and took his time in ensuring that she had her pleasure before he took his own. They had never grown bored with each other because there always seemed to be something for them to talk about, whether it be about the latest bestseller or even, heaven forbid, politics. They had shared so much more than a job; they had shared their dreams and their souls. Mari doubted, arrogantly, there was another couple like Reid and Alicia in the entire world. Mari hadn't had any lovers in the past few years, by choice. Each time she thought a man might be the lover she was looking for something went wrong and she backed out in the nick of time. After the second time this happened she had decided she was better off living the life of a nun.

She stirred in the water, reaching for the wash-cloth and running the soft cotton lazily over her arms and legs. When she reached her breasts she thought of Reid, the way he would cup the round globes, tease the nipples with his thumbs then take each one into his mouth and suckle like a babe. But this thought only got her into trouble. Her nipples tightened in reaction and an ache began at her breasts and wove a white-hot path down to her belly. She shifted her legs in an effort to dispel the ache but it only intensified as the silky water hit the ultrasensitive area. She moaned softly as visions of Reid making love to Alicia flashed before her eyes—a vision that was just as potent as the dream she'd had days earlier. Swearing under her breath, she abruptly stood up and headed for the shower. Right about now a nice cold shower would be just the ticket.

She had just stepped out of the shower and wrapped a towel around her when the telephone rang. Thinking it was Reid, she smiled at the idea of him calling her when he would see her within the next hour. She practically chirped when she picked up the phone.

"Getting impatient, aren't we?" she caroled.

"I wouldn't say that's the word I would use." Lucas spoke in his usual harsh monotone. "You never listen, do you?"

Mari froze. "Listen to what, Lucas?" She wasn't going to allow him to intimidate her any more.

"Don't be a smartass, Mari. You know exactly what I'm talking about. What is this crap about you going out fishing with Reid and spending just about every waking moment with him during the past few days? I'm surprised the two of you haven't fallen into bed yet. Which one is holding out?"

Her fingers tightened on the cord. "You bastard, you're still spying on us. I told you before that I wouldn't give anything away and I haven't. I'm sure you would have known firsthand if Reid had found out the truth because he would travel to Washington immediately and kill you."

Lucas didn't answer right away, probably because he knew she spoke the truth. If Reid found out about Mari/Alicia, he would indeed blame Lucas and punish him accordingly.

"Don't even think about telling him, Mari. That would only mean that his life would be in as great a danger as yours. Inquiries are still being made about Alicia, you know. I would suggest, my dear, that you watch your back at all times."

By now she was the one who was coldly furious. "That's your job, *my dear*, I'm just the patsy." Then it hit her with the force of a sledgehammer. "That's it, isn't it? I'm bait to capture those bastards."

"You are no such thing," he replied firmly. "While you are no longer an active member of our . . . group, you are still one of us and will be taken care of accordingly. I just want to warn you that the time may come when someone will track you down in order to see exactly how much you remember."

Mari closed her eyes. Harsh guttural sounds vibrated in her head, printed letters danced before

87

her lids. The information she had been sent to steal had been burned into her memory, but when the time came for her to retrieve the names and places, she had discovered that she couldn't remember. Due to the severe trauma she had suffered in prison her subconscious chose to bury the facts. To this day all that rose to the surface were the vague memories that brought about her nightmares.

"I don't want you to call me again, Lucas," she said slowly. "I don't intend to tell Reid anything and, as I said before, I won't give in to you. You've stolen the past few years from us and I refuse to allow you to cheat us any longer." She replaced the receiver in the cradle with great care before collapsing on the bed. She wrapped her arms around her to stave off the cold seeping into her bones. Damn Lucas for bringing up that terrorist group! Surely he knew just thinking about them gave her the shivers. All the time that had elapsed since then still hadn't taken away the fear that haunted her so many nights.

By the time Mari met Reid in the restaurant she felt more like her old self. Or was it her new self? Sometimes she wasn't sure. Many days she gave up trying to figure out exactly who she was. Of course, if anyone asked she would smile and say she was Mari Janette Chandler, aged thirty-two, born in Charlotte, North Carolina, attended high school there and college in Atlanta. If anyone cared to check, they would learn Mari was an excellent student, had been a member of the pep and photography clubs, was a cheerleader, and had an A —

average. She worked as a secretary in a law office until she received a legacy from her parents that enabled her to open her lingerie shop, Naughty and Nice. She belonged to the Chamber of Commerce and several women's clubs and owned a lovely three-story home on the outskirts of town. Some may have thought the house was too large for a single woman but it suited her just fine. Yet there were still days when Mari Chandler didn't feel like Mari, but she didn't feel like Alicia either. She supposed she should have continued seeing the psychiatrist Lucas referred her to, but she hadn't felt comfortable around the man so she stopped seeing him after several sessions. If anyone was going to solve her identity crisis, she would have to do it herself.

"Hey, come back to earth." Reid waved his hand in front of her face.

Mari blinked and smiled. "Sorry, I guess I sort of blanked out for a moment."

"What sent you into outer space?"

She shrugged. "Oh, just thinking that my vacation will be over before I know it and I'll be back to the old grind." And Reid will be back to running all over Europe, which is what he does best. Well, what he does second best, she amended silently. Alicia had always teased Reid saying he had two talents; thanks to one of them, he would never have any problem seducing an agent from the other side to learn information. Alicia figured that most women would gladly tell him anything he wanted to know. She had also warned him that if he ever did try that particular technique, she would make sure he wouldn't have the inclination to do so again! Just as abruptly as the thoughts entered Mari's head she swept them out again. It was times like this when she was grateful that she had been trained to keep her thoughts to herself. If Reid had any idea what was going on in her head, he would probably demand to know the entire story and she wouldn't be able to tell him anything. Not only because of her promise to Lucas but because she still couldn't bear talking about that time. It still hurt too much.

"What would you say to taking one of those bus tours to the ruins tomorrow?" Reid suggested. "If you take your camera you'll get some great pictures."

"Have you been there before?" she asked, playing with the delicate lemon souffle she had ordered for dessert. Thanks to Lucas's telephone call her appetite had disappeared and she had only been able to toy with her food.

"A long time ago," he murmured, staring into his coffee cup. "A very long time ago."

Mari chose not to force the issue. She had memories also and preferred to keep them under wraps as much as Reid did.

They finished their meal in silence and when Reid suggested they walk along the beach, Mari agreed. She had no wish to sit in one of the lounges and listen to music and drink for the rest of the evening. The solitude the beach would offer would be just the thing. She cursed Lucas for upsetting her.

"Something's wrong," Reid commented as they

walked along the water's edge. Mari had slipped off her sandals, grateful her legs were tanned dark enough that she didn't have to worry about taking off stockings.

"Call it near-the-end-of-vacation blues."

"You don't seem like the type to depress easily; besides, what's to worry? Your vacation's barely begun."

"I certainly wouldn't consider myself Little Mary Sunshine. I get cranky and bitchy just like everyone else. In fact, there are some days when my assistant suggests I stay in the back of the shop while she plays lady of the manor, so to speak."

Reid smiled. "When does that happen?"

"When a very stout lady comes in and requests a very filmy negligee in a size medium when it's only too obvious that an extra large would be a tight fit. Denise is very good at steering the lady to an appropriate item without offending her. I have a lot of trouble understanding why someone would refuse to recognize their true size and buy clothing they'll never be able to wear or be very uncomfortable in. Many times I can be discreet but there are other times when I just want to point out the mistake they're making."

Reid nodded, glad to hear she had more spirit than she had betrayed in the beginning. So this little kitten had claws after all. The first time she had betrayed more than her usual calm exterior was that afternoon on the boat when she pleaded with him to release the marlin. This confession was the second time. He was tempted to escort her to his bungalow and find out even more about her, but fishing had left him more tired than he expected and he doubted he could give her all she deserved. But he wasn't worried. There was always another day and another night. He'd make sure to get plenty of rest tonight. He guessed he was growing older faster than he thought. How was James Bond able to chase spies all day and seduce women all night when he was having enough trouble just keeping up with the lady walking next to him? If Alicia were there she would tease him unmercifully that he better increase his vitamin E intake. That was the first time he had thought of her without the accompanying pain. It looked like his idea of releasing her spirit was working. He also felt that he had Mari to thank for that. He reached out and grasped her hand, lacing his fingers through hers. Her skin was cool and soft against his own rough palm. It was too dark to see her face clearly, but he could still visualize the slightly rounded contours of her face, the clear green eyes that held secrets he wanted to delve into as fully as he wanted to delve into her body. There was the soft lyrical drawl that could soothe any man's emotional pain; indeed, he felt better just being around her. He hadn't forgotten her response when he had kissed her. He might not be able to hope for more tonight but he was certainly going to kiss her good night even if leaving her for his lonely bed killed him!

"Tell me about your travels, Reid," Mari requested softly. She already knew what yarn he would spin but she needed to hear him speak. She wanted to convince herself that it truly was him walking beside her and not some dream she would eventually wake up from. How many times over the past few years had she dreamed of being with Reid only to wake up crying, knowing that it would never happen? Well, it finally had, and as she told Lucas, she was going to take full advantage of the time she was blessed with. All too soon she would return to Charlotte and have only memories from these halcyon days to live with. She told herself sternly to snap out of her doldrums before Reid sensed her sorrow and questioned it again. She doubted that he believed her answer about end of vacation blues. It had sounded lame even to her, but it was the only thing she could think of at the time. The days of coming up with quick, plausible answers had been over a long time and she was just plain out of practice. Mari bent down to pick up a handful of sand.

"What do you think, were these grains part of a large boulder millions of years ago or an ancient dinosaur?" she mused, watching the sand flow between her fingertips.

"How about the ancestor of the Loch Ness monster?"

"Then that ancestor did an awful lot of traveling to get here all the way from Scotland."

"Maybe he just wanted a warmer climate."

"Or a nice tan. Do you think his demise was due to a bad case of *turista?*"

Reid grinned at the mischievous light in Mari's eyes. "I guess no one told him not to drink the water."

Mari laughed and accepted his helping hand as she rose to her feet. But her laugh died as Reid's hands tightened on her arms. He looked down into her upturned face with an expression that was taut with emotion. Without saying a word, his head lowered until their lips brushed. She angled her head to one side for easier access. Her tongue flickered out to taste the man she had loved for years. The man Alicia had had to give up, but Mari wasn't about to give him up just yet. This was her chance and she wasn't about to let it go. She heard his sharp indrawn breath as her tongue grazed his lower lip. Feeling bolder, she closed her teeth over that same lip and drew it into her mouth.

Reid's arms encircled her shoulders and drew her fully against him. He widened his stance so that she could feel his arousal pulsing against her belly. With a deep groan born in his throat, he took over the kiss. His tongue thrust roughly into her eager mouth demanding all she could give him. This was not a time for tender exploration, he needed her too much. He was beginning to think that he wasn't all that tired after all. He felt her breasts press against his chest and he wanted to open her blouse and feel the bare softness in his hands. He wanted to see if they were as pearly white as he envisioned and if the tips were pink or dusky rose. Since he couldn't touch her bare skin he settled for kneading the full globe through the thin creamy silk. It was enough to cause all his earlier good intentions to fly right out the window.

Mari moaned as dark passion surrounded her. She was at the point where she wouldn't have

94

protested if Reid had drawn her down onto the sand and made love to her in front of the entire world. All she knew was that the man she loved was kissing and caressing her as if there were no tomorrow. Indeed, for her time was passing all too quickly. She rubbed herself against him and dug her fingers into his shoulders, silently asking for more. And Reid just might have given it to her if a faint sound in the distance hadn't roused her to sanity.

"No." She moaned, pushing him away so suddenly that he stumbled. Tears sprang into her eyes as she stared at his face, still dark with the passion they had shared. "I can't. I just can't." She turned and ran up the sand to her bungalow.

Reid remained standing there watching her retreat. He wanted to feel angry at her for running away but he had seen the stark fear in her eyes and knew that something had triggered it. One moment she had been murmuring sweet things in his ear and giving an excellent impression of a woman who wanted a man to make love to her. The next she was running away. He intended to find out what had gone wrong.

Mari ran to her room fumbling with the lock as her trembling fingers tried to hold the key steady. Tears were coursing down her cheeks as she tossed her purse and key onto the bed. She was beginning to regret her idea of coming here. Perhaps it would have been better if she had taken Lucas up on his offer. It was getting more difficult to resist Reid when she wanted so desperately to feel his naked body against hers. She collapsed in the chair holding her hands against her face as she gave in to the sorrow that had plagued her all evening. She was so lost in her tears that she didn't hear the soft *click* of the door opening and closing.

"A woman has never cried before just because I've kissed her." Reid's dry voice came as a shock.

Mari jumped, looking up to see him standing over her. He showed no sympathy for her distress.

"How did you get in here?" she demanded. "Oh, I see. You're not a construction engineer at all, you're a cat burglar and very adept in picking locks, right? Well, if you're looking for valuables here you've come to the wrong place." Her only defense was a caustic offense.

"If that's what you want to believe I won't stop you. I just want to know why you were more than willing for me to make love to you then suddenly changed your mind. I didn't think you were a tease."

Mari flushed at the accusation. "I'm not," she replied in a low voice. "But making love on a beach where anyone could stumble upon us isn't my idea of a good time. I came here to relax, not to cut a notch on my bedpost."

Reid's eyes narrowed. He hadn't expected her to accuse him of disregarding her wishes. Although he had been the one to deepen the embrace, she certainly hadn't fought him. He naturally would have thought she wanted it that way. Was there some reason she shied away from the ultimate possession? Had a man hurt her badly in the past? Was she afraid of experiencing that same hurt again? Or was it because of her fiancé's death that she had trouble relating intimately to a man? True, he couldn't promise more than a few days' pleasure before he would return to Washington and then on to Europe. But he doubted he would easily forget her. In fact, he wanted to contact her when he returned to the States. A tiny suspicious part of his brain asked if that wasn't what she really wanted.

Mari sat there in her misery, damning Reid for coming to Mexico the same time as she did and damning Lucas for forcing her to live a lie. And because of this she would have to lie again.

"I—ah—I told you before, I'm just finally beginning to get over my fiancé's death." She spoke with just the right touch of reluctance. "It was a very difficult time for me." She kept her eyes lowered. It wasn't an original story, but it should be effective.

Reid studied her downcast features. He wanted to believe her. It would certainly account for her being so gunshy around him. Being close to a man again had probably brought a very painful past back to her.

"Reid, perhaps you should look for someone else if you want a vacation affair," she suggested. "It's just not something for me."

He remained standing in front of her, his hands jammed in his pockets.

"I'll check on those tours first thing in the morning to see if we can get on one," he said finally. "I'll let you know." He turned back to the door. "Sometimes you have to forget the pain one person caused you or you'll miss out on something that could be very beautiful." He opened the door. "Oh, and lock it next time." He left her just as quietly as he arrived.

CHAPTER FIVE

The moment Reid left Mari his doubts about her returned full force. By the time he entered his bungalow he had made his decision. He took a quick shower and then made several phone calls. To gather the information he required, he called in just about every favor he was owed. He also had to ensure that word of his curiosity wouldn't reach important ears, namely, Lucas's.

It took a few hours but it was worth it, for he discovered a few things.

"Your Mari Chandler has a very nice background, ol' buddy," Thorson, his contact in Data Processing, told him.

"Then she is working for someone else?" He cursed himself for missing that vital bit identifying her as the enemy.

"She's clean as a whistle, in fact, too clean. She doesn't even have a parking ticket to her name."

"You mean she's under our protection?" Reid guessed. The agency often gave witnesses or valuable informants who might have to go underground complete new identities and found them safe places to live.

"Maybe."

"Maybe? Come on, Thorson, you handle the records for the relocations. If anyone knew, you would."

"I may handle the records but she must be a special case I don't know about. Or she just may be what she seems. She appears to be a hard-working businesswoman who's on vacation." Thorson reeled off facts and figures that Reid could have cared less about. But Reid understood what his friend meant—there were few personal facts about the lady. She was too perfect.

"Hey, Reid, maybe we've been in this business too long. We suspect someone just because they're too normal. I met this dynamite lady a few weeks ago and I thought about dropping her when she mentioned she studied Russian in college."

"Suspicion is the name of the game, pal," Reid countered. "You know that. Look, thanks for doing this for me. I owe you one."

"I'll pick out the bar when you return to D.C. and you can pick out the ladies. You seem to have better luck with them than I do. As for this Chandler lady, you know one of the boss's commandments—thou shalt not fall for a woman." He stopped and uttered a pungent curse. "God, Reid, I'm sorry. You know me and my fast mouth."

"Hey, don't worry about it," he said wearily. "It's been a long time."

Reid hung up and stared at the wall across from the bed. From the beginning he had wondered about Mari, and now after talking to Thorson, he wondered even more.

He had quit smoking a year ago but right now he'd sell his soul for a cigarette. Maybe he could think more clearly if he was drawing that wonderful acrid smoke into his lungs. The more he thought about it the more desperate he became for a smoke.

He did without the cigarettes, but as soon as the clock displayed a decent hour the following morning he called Mari and asked to postpone their trip. He didn't bother to give her a reason.

Reid wasn't the only one who utilized the department's computer to find out about Mari Chandler. Another man who monitored computer activity noticed a request regarding the same woman he was curious about. Though he didn't have the security clearance to enter the classified files, that didn't stop him from finding out what he needed to know. He was an expert at breaking into the supposedly inviolate. Bringing up the file on Mari Chandler was a piece of cake. After copying down all the information he could learn, he left the computer room as unobtrusively as he had entered then made sure he was far away from the office building before finding a pay phone and calling the man who had promised to pay him well for the information. He was certain he had found the woman his superiors were looking for. If he was wrong, there would be no second chance.

The man he called was very interested in hearing about Reid's trip to Mexico and his sudden interest in a woman there who was about the same age as Alicia Brookes would have been. Based on this information, he decided it would be profitable to send someone to Mexico with the orders to notify him if she did turn out to be Alicia Brookes. Killing her was to be his joyful task.

He knows something, Mari told herself as she replaced the receiver after Reid called her to cancel their date. *He either knows something for sure or strongly suspects.*

Alicia had known Reid as well as she had known herself. He had made many friends within the department and always knew exactly whom to contact if he needed information.

At first Mari panicked, wondering if she should call Lucas and confess her thoughts. Luckily, sanity took over before she could dial the number. If she told Lucas of her fears he would immediately pull her out of there, even if he had to personally carry her out kicking and screaming. No, she couldn't call him.

Mari paced the floor. She hadn't handled this very well. She had promised Lucas that she wouldn't reveal her identity, but that didn't mean Reid might not learn the truth from another source. What would happen then? Would he be happy that Alicia hadn't died? No, he would more than likely be angry over the deception, and Mari would receive the brunt of the blame.

Mari buried her face in her hands. Reid couldn't be angry with her. Oh, sure, he'd be furious and he would probably direct that anger at Lucas for beginning the lies. But he would also be angry with Mari for continuing it. And she would lose him again. No. She had to pull herself together long enough to finish her charade and return home. There would be time enough for self-recrimination when she was back in North Carolina.

Reid sat at the small table, a tray holding a coffeepot and empty plate pushed to one side. The sheet of paper he studied was covered with neat printing. All of it held his thoughts regarding Mari Chandler. When something perplexed him he usually sat down and wrote out his thoughts and generally discovered a solution. This time he wasn't so lucky. The pros and cons seemed more a mumbo jumbo than the crisp facts he was so used to dealing with.

He wanted to believe that she wasn't planted there to catch his attention. After all, she isn't a skinny blonde. He wanted to believe that she was a woman who really wasn't as complicated as she sometimes came across. So why would someone with an accent as Southern as fried chicken and a smile like morning sunshine have such haunted eyes when she looked at him? And what had put that look in them? What was so special about her that all he could think of was undressing her and taking her into his bed for a very long and pleasurable time? The funny thing was that he was certain that it was more than physical attraction he felt for her.

He muttered under his breath. With a flick of a match the paper was consumed by flickering orange flame until only ashes floated down into the glass ashtray. No one would ever know about the suspicions he harbored.

Mari spent a day and night guaranteed to give even the hardiest person ulcers. She restlessly mapped out the room with her feet, stopping only to order coffee from room service. It was past midnight when she finally huddled in bed, the bathroom light on to keep away the night shadows. She waited for Reid to barge in, demanding an explanation from Alicia. When dawn arrived without any visitors she fell into an uneasy sleep.

Mari heard bells ringing. Correction, one bell ringing. She raised leaden eyelids and stared at the phone as if it could answer itself. She doubted she had the energy to roll over and pick it up. But the ornery beige telephone refused to stop ringing.

" 'Lo?" she croaked.

"Mari?" Reid's voice was sharp. "Are you all right?"

She yawned. "What time is it?"

"Six."

"In the morning?"

"Yep."

Mari groaned. "I'm sorry, but Mari is unable to take your call. At the tone please leave a message and she will get back to you later, much later." She hung up and rolled over pulling her pillow over her head.

Luckily, Reid waited two hours before knocking on Mari's door. She pulled it open and peered out.

"Why are you punishing me?" She turned away and groped for her robe.

104

"Your answering service said to get back to you later. This is later."

"My answering service said *I* would get back to *you* later." She yawned. "Look, you cancelled yesterday, fine. Something came up and my feelings aren't hurt. I don't need someone showing up at my door at the crack of dawn." She knew exactly what part she had to play: that of the woman with wounded feelings who refused to show how she felt. After all, she was only dallying with the man, right? Well, it always sounded good to her when she read scenes like that in a book.

"The crack of dawn appeared a long time ago," Reid corrected. "Besides, you have exactly forty minutes to get dressed before we leave."

"Leave?" *Bad, Mari,* she thought, *now you sound like a parrot.*

"There's a tour bus leaving for the ruins at nine. If you can be dressed in forty minutes you'll have enough time for a cup of coffee and maybe some toast," Reid tempted. It had taken many hours before he came to his decision. He wasn't going to be able to put aside his suspicions because they were a part of his life. But he would give her a chance. As Thorson said, she might just be normal. The trouble was that after so many years living in shadows and alleys, he wouldn't know normal if it hit him on the head. He wanted to apologize to her for his rude behavior earlier but he wasn't very good at apologies either. The best he could do was sign them up for this morning's tour and appear on Mari's doorstep, hoping to charm her into going with him before she had a chance to slam the door in his face. Luckily, she was half asleep when he showed up; his surprise visit left her off balance long enough to get him inside the bungalow before she had time to wake up fully and order him out. Which he would have richly deserved. Thank God he was used to thinking on his feet. Now all he had to do was make sure she was willing to go on that tour with him.

She pushed her tousled hair away from her face and wished she could conjure up a temper and order him from her door. Too bad Mari didn't have a temper. Alicia would have sent Reid packing with a few choice words uttered in several languages. Oh, yes, when Alicia had gone on a rampage she did it with style. She had a temper hot enough to rival the Irish and the Italians, but it cooled just as quickly. She never believed in carrying grudges; they took up too much time.

"If you want me ready in time I suggest you wait for me in the coffee shop with my breakfast waiting," she said finally. So Reid hadn't found out the truth after all. She never doubted that he had checked on her. It was part of the game. But obviously Lucas had her records as clean as possible. She knew it didn't mean she didn't have to be cautious; Reid still wouldn't drop his guard and she hadn't missed seeing the questions in his eyes when he entered the room. As she vowed after she first saw Reid, she would just take one day at a time.

Reid's body relaxed. She wasn't going to throw him out after all. He glanced down at his watch. "Shall I be crass and time you?"

She stood up and ushered him outside. "I wouldn't suggest it unless you want that very nice watch to end up at the bottom of the ocean," she said sweetly before she closed the door after him.

Mari raced to get ready. She practically ran in and out of the shower and washed her hair with the speed of light. How she applied her makeup correctly and dressed in coordinated colors she wasn't sure. When she left her bungalow thirty-four minutes later she was dressed in a pale-aqua and lavender striped knit top and aqua shorts and comfortable sandals. She reached the coffee shop to find Reid seated in a rear booth with a carafe of coffee on the table. She took the seat opposite him, and the moment she sat down the waitress set a plate of bacon and eggs in front of her.

"I just wanted toast," Mari protested, looking at the filled plate. "This is too much for me to eat."

"We're probably going to be walking a lot and you're going to need all the energy you can get," he informed her. "So at least eat what you can."

Mari sighed but did manage to eat most of the eggs and all of the bacon. Reid finished up her toast and led her outside to the blue-and-white dusty bus waiting in front of the hotel.

"Are you sure this thing can drive farther than two miles down the road?" Mari asked under her breath, studying the beat-up vehicle that looked as if it hadn't been used since World War I.

"It makes two trips a day," Reid assured her.

"I'm sure it does, thanks to the passengers getting out and pushing," she muttered, climbing aboard with Reid behind her. He gestured to a seat near the middle and she slid onto the cracked vinyl seat. "It's amazing how a luxury hotel can allow this relic on their grounds."

The bus was half full when the guide boarded and in thickly accented English welcomed the passengers and explained what their tour would entail.

Mari sat back against the seat, prepared to relax as much as possible, but a prickling sensation skittered across her shoulder blades. She didn't look to the right or left but she was positive someone was watching her, someone who wanted to hurt her. That sixth sense should have died with Alicia, but it wasn't something that could be thrown away like an old dress. Her stomach began to churn with old remembered fears, but she forced them down deep. She blamed it on a sleepless night. There was no one there to hurt her. Besides, Reid was with her. Wait a minute, what if someone was after Reid? She could only pray he felt something too because she couldn't afford to blow her cover no matter how badly she wanted to.

Reid also felt an aura of danger in the bus. He had felt it much sooner than Mari since his senses were more finely honed than hers. Why he noticed the feeling there and not in the coffee shop, where it would seem more likely, was what he couldn't understand. He stared forward into the driver's rearview mirror looking at the reflected passengers. All looked pretty normal, mainly couples except for two elderly women who were probably retired schoolteachers. There was one man in the back he would have liked a better look at but he wore dark glasses and had a hat pulled down over his eyes as if he intended to nap during the half-hour drive out to the ruins. Reid would just have to make sure to look him over when he disembarked. The strange thing was that he didn't feel that the danger lurking nearby was directed at him. Hell, he'd been stalked enough times to know the difference. So, who was tailing whom? His first thought was Mari, but it didn't make any sense. Unless Thorson was right and she was under their agency's protection and her new identity had been found out. He thought about quizzing her about it that evening but knew that if she was under their care, he wouldn't find out a thing. He'd just have to wait and see what transpired during the day. Maybe he was just a little too paranoid. But then his sixth sense had never been wrong before.

"This man's jokes are very bad," Mari leaned over to murmur in Reid's ear as she braced herself for the jolting ride. If she didn't hang on, she was afraid she'd end up bounced right out the open window.

"Maybe so, but he does have style."

"I wouldn't exactly call it that." She resisted the urge to beg Reid to be careful. As long as she kept talking, she wouldn't start thinking about the fright coursing through her body.

Reid took her hand and placed it palm down on his thigh. "Look at it this way. At least we didn't have to pay a fifty-dollar cover charge to listen to him."

Mari groaned and laughed at the same time.

"I'm not sure that makes me feel better." Without thinking, she scratched his skin lightly and felt the muscles tense under her touch.

"Honey, can't you even wait until we get back to the hotel?" Reid said in a stage whisper. "I'm still so tired after last night."

Mari's face reddened as she heard the soft laughter around her from the people who had obviously overheard Reid's remarks. She tried to jerk her hand away from his hold but he refused to give it up.

"Let me have my fun," he whispered, pausing to nibble on her earlobe.

"Not at my expense."

"Don't worry, I'll let you get even with me later."

Mari could think of a great many ways to get even and all of them made her cheeks flame. The temperature was warm enough already but it rose even higher around her. With Reid keeping hold of her hand and using his fingers to write naughty messages across its back, she forgot about her earlier fears.

When the bus arrived at the ruins and the passengers disembarked, Reid looked around for the mysterious man from the back but couldn't find him. Now he was really worried. If the man was merely a tourist, why didn't he stay with the group? He resolved to remain on his guard for the rest of the day just in case anything did happen. He would also have to make sure that Mari didn't get caught in any crossfire.

Mari felt equally apprehensive. She couldn't get

rid of the feeling that something might happen that day. She remembered Lucas's warnings that if the terrorists were positive she was still alive, they might strike back at her through those she loved. What if Reid ended up the victim? Her entire body rejected the thought of Reid lying near death in the dust. He was too smart to allow anyone to get the drop on him! How many times had he cheated death in much worse situations than this? But death might win the game this time. Even with the blistering heat of the day, Mari felt cold. She resisted the idea of wrapping her arms around her chilled body. Instead she called upon her inner strength and forced herself to listen to the guide's dissertation about the ancient Indian ruins where many rituals had taken place.

"Virgin sacrifices," Reid whispered lasciviously, earning a dark glare from her. "Fertility rites." Mari rolled her eyes and tried to look disgusted, but it was difficult when she could imagine what the fertility rites would entail. Hm, Reid, wearing only a colorful loincloth, his tanned chest bare and burnished with sweat from the hot sun. She wondered how long fertility rites would last. Mari shook her head. It had to be the tropical sun making her delirious. Maybe that was why she had felt so uneasy on the bus, especially since Reid didn't appear to be worried about anything. She allowed him to take her hand as they wandered about the stone ruins of several temples and inspected the intricate carvings.

"How can we think these people were barbarians when they created such beauty?" Reid mused, studying one stone carving of two maidens carrying trays of food to a group of warriors then moving on to another where priests worshipped one of their gods.

"Perhaps we think so because we don't believe in offering the life of one of our virgins to the gods or dropping her into a deep well as a sacrifice to ensure a good harvest," Mari replied, resisting the urge to turn around and scan the surrounding jungle. Someone was watching her, she was certain of it. And by the vibrations going through her body, she was positive her peeping Tom wasn't one of Lucas's men. Had they finally learned her identity? Had her time finally run out?

"Hey!" Reid looked down at Mari's hand, which was crushing his. "No offense, but I'm kind of attached to that hand and you're cutting off the circulation."

"Oh, sorry." She hastily loosened her grip. "I guess I was so caught up in the past I didn't realize what I was doing."

Reid thought differently. The sensation of being followed was back and while he didn't like to think so, he couldn't help but wonder if Mari didn't have something to do with it.

"Let's catch up with the rest of the group," he said abruptly, pulling on her hand.

For the next hour they walked around the temples and listened to their guide discuss legends. Mari listened with rapt attention and didn't notice when Reid silently moved away. He had decided that this was as good a time as any to investigate the area and see if he could find the missing passenger. As long as Mari stayed with the group she would be safe.

Reid skirted the jungle growth looking for the slightest clue until he was out of sight.

It took Mari a few moments to realize Reid was no longer standing next to her. She looked around but didn't see him anywhere. Worried, she eased away from the group to go look for him. Mari searched between the temples, picking her way among the scattered stones.

"Reid?" she called out softly. "Reid, are you here?" Suddenly the parrots shrieking overhead stopped, all the usual jungle sounds were silent. She felt as if she were the last person left in the world, it was so quiet.

"Alicia!" The hissing voice was from the past, out of a nightmare.

It took every ounce of courage for her not to acknowledge the voice. She pretended she hadn't heard. Her blood chilled each time the voice called out Alicia's name. She wanted nothing more than to scream out to her tormentor to leave her alone, but she couldn't give herself away. If she did she would sign her death certificate.

"We know all about you, Alicia," the voice taunted from the jungle. "And we want you back because we miss you so much. Don't you miss us? We used to have such fun together."

"Hey, buddy, there's no one else here," she finally called out in a voice that she couldn't allow to sound frightened. "If you want your girl friend so badly I suggest you look somewhere else."

"Very good, Alicia. People just might believe

you are not her. Just remember, we know differently." A rustle of leaves and she knew he was gone.

Mari kept a very tight hold on her composure when she found Reid a few minutes later and strove to remain calm during the trip back to the hotel. When Reid commented on her pale features, she blamed them on the heat. She was so caught up in her own fears she didn't see him look around and notice the bus was missing a passenger. When they reached the hotel, Mari begged off having a drink by saying she wanted nothing more than a cool shower and to lie down before dinner. After agreeing to meet him later, she hurried to her bungalow. The moment she reached the safety of her room, she checked every corner and under every lamp. Finding it as clean as when she left it, she stumbled into the bathroom and was violently ill. Then she pulled off her damp clothing and practically crawled into the shower to wash away the sweat of fear. Mari almost used up the bar of soap cleansing every inch of her body, and when finished she scrubbed her hair thoroughly. After her shower, Mari headed straight for the phone and dialed Lucas's number. She uttered the appropriate code words and waited for the line to be switched over several times before Lucas's calm voice echoed in her ear.

"I was tailed today," she said crisply.

"Were you approached?"

"A name was called out." She knew enough not to say any names out loud. "I was on a tour of some local ruins when it happened."

"I don't suppose you saw the person?"

Mari was very close to losing her temper. "No, I didn't see anyone! I was too busy trying not to have a nervous breakdown."

"Mari, you're distraught. Might I suggest a warm bath and a glass of brandy."

She was about to suggest what he could do with the brandy and warm bath when she heard a knock at her door. "I have to go. Someone's at my door. I want you to find out who was here, Lucas."

"Was Reid with you?" he asked.

"No, but James Bond and Sherlock Holmes were along to keep the party rolling." With that she slammed the telephone down. "I'm coming!" She headed for the door, which fairly vibrated under the persistent pounding. Mari's mood wasn't pleasant when she pulled the door open. "What do you want?"

Reid blinked at her rude greeting. He held up a wine bottle and two glasses. "I thought you might need this."

Mari wilted under his smile. She stepped back to allow him to enter then realized she was wearing only a silky robe that clung to her damp body and her wet hair was curling around her face. "I'm not exactly dressed for company," she murmured, edging toward the bathroom where she hoped to make a few major repairs. She must look like a fright; she certainly sounded like one!

Reid dropped the bottle and glasses on the bed and grasped her wrist with split-second timing.

"There's nothing at all wrong with the way you look," he said, pulling her closer to him. When she

115

stood in front of him he threaded his hands through her hair and gently pulled her head back for his kiss.

Mari couldn't remember ever receiving such a gentle kiss. Reid's slightly parted lips floated over her mouth and along her jawline and up to her forehead. Her eyes drifted closed and she lost herself in the warm sensation of his touch.

"Let me taste you," he said huskily, moving back to the temptation of her mouth. He rubbed his tongue over her lower lip until it lowered for his possession. Even then he wasn't as forceful as he wanted to be. Each touch was soft, almost childlike, if such a thing were possible from such a virile man.

Mari slipped her arms around Reid's waist and hugged him tightly. She felt as if she could hold onto him for the rest of her life and never get tired of him. And she certainly wasn't going to complain as long as he kept kissing her.

Reid's thumbs pressed lightly against her spine, moving up and down in a caressing motion.

"As much as I'd like to continue doing this, I think I better quit while I'm ahead," he murmured against her lips.

"Are you sure?" she asked in her most sultry voice, moving her hips against his.

Reid groaned as he slowly disengaged himself from her embrace. "Against my better judgment, yes, I am sure." Though he moved away to a safe distance, that didn't hide his arousal from her. Mari hid her smile of triumph. Reid busied himself opening the wine and pouring it into the two glasses. "It's already been established that I want to make love to you and I'm pretty sure that you're receptive to the idea," he said bluntly. "But I still feel the time isn't right. Admittedly, neither of us will be here all that much longer and so I hope you will understand when I say that I won't be patient for too much longer." He handed her one of the glasses and held his up for a toast.

Mari's stomach contracted. The idea of Reid making love to her was very tempting, but she knew it would also be very dangerous. As much as she hated the idea, she just might have to cut her vacation short and run back to Charlotte before it was too late. Oh, Reid would be angry at her defection, but she doubted he would bother chasing after someone who proved to be so troublesome.

"To the rest of our vacation." She managed to smile as she held her own glass up.

The swarthy man found an unused telephone in the airport and quickly made his call.

"Is she the one?" was the first question put to him when his employer answered the phone and he had identified himself.

He paused. "I am not sure. I did as you told me and called out the name and said what you told me to say, but she gave no indication she knew the person."

"You idiot! Did you expect her to smile and answer you? She was a trained agent. Of course she would not say anything. But did her manner indicate she was the one?" he asked harshly.

He paused again. He was positive that the

wrong answer could cost him his life. "I think that Rashid was wrong with his information, sir. She does not look at all like the agent or sound like her."

The man cursed long and loud. It was clear he didn't appreciate being thwarted again. "You have a plane reservation?"

"Yes, for New York, as I was instructed."

"Change it. You will fly to Washington, D.C., and talk to Rashid. Oh, and Khira"—he used the man's code name—"I suggest that you make sure that Rashid cannot talk to anyone else about this. I will personally look into this matter further. If it turns out that you have made an error . . ." He left his threat unsaid. It was easy enough to guess what would happen to him.

Khira gulped. Oh, yes, he knew exactly what would happen. No matter how fast he ran or how far he traveled, he would not be able to escape the clutches of the organization and the man people called Black Death. Like the plague of so many years ago, he left no one alive.

CHAPTER SIX

During the next few days Reid showed Mari in many ways how much he desired her, but he indicated he would also look for a sign from her. And while Mari would like nothing more than to stay in bed with Reid for the next hundred years, she knew it would be a major mistake. At the same time she felt there was someone watching her even though she didn't see anyone suspicious around the hotel. Of course, if her private spy was good at his job she wouldn't notice anything, especially since her skills weren't what they used to be.

In the meantime she and Reid parted each evening feeling extremely frustrated. What she couldn't understand was why he would put up with it when there were so many willing women around. One evening she even suggested he might be happier if he found someone else.

"Yeah, but would her hair smell like lemons and would she smell like springtime?" he teased her, planting another mind-blowing kiss on her lips.

"If that's all you require I'll lend the lady my shampoo and perfume," she retorted, trying to pull out of his arms without any success.

"Ah, but she still wouldn't be you." Reid laughed, pulling her up against him for another possessive kiss.

By then Mari was past protesting anything. When Reid finally left her at her door she was walking on air and delighted at the prospect of their going off for a picnic the following day. Mari had gone shopping for a special outfit and invested in a very becoming bikini. For long moments she had stared at a scarlet confection hanging in the boutique window and thought how good the string bikini would have looked on Alicia's slim figure. In fact, it would have even looked good with Mari's curves, but Mari didn't have the nerve to wear it. She turned away, reminding herself that the suit was more Alicia's style, and settled for a dark-blue, red, and black diagonally striped bikini with a bandeau top. Paired with an off-white gauzy pullover top and tan shorts, she felt very sexy.

When Mari met Reid at the boat landing, the expression in his eyes when he saw the outline of the suit under the semisheer top told her that he thought very much the same thing.

"Where are we going?" she asked once Reid had started the motor to the small boat and steered it out of the protected bay.

"To the other side of the island," he replied, shouting over the roar of the engine. "Manuel told me about a cove there that's perfect for snorkeling."

"I don't know how to snorkel," she confessed.

He flashed her a broad grin. "Don't worry, I'll teach you. There's nothing to it."

It took them almost half an hour to reach the cove, but the moment Mari saw it she knew the long ride had been more than worth it. She jumped out into the water and helped Reid pull the boat onto the beach. Then she waited as he drew out the large wicker basket.

Mari looked around at the empty expanse of white sandy beach and the lush green jungle several hundred yards above that.

"It's like being on a deserted island," she cried with delight, spinning around in a circle her arms held out from her sides.

Reid looked up, smiling at her open laughter and happiness. He realized it was the first time he had seen her truly relaxed. For the past few days she appeared tense at times and had a habit of looking over her shoulder. Had the man on the bus been there to keep an eye on her? He hadn't seen the man since that day and might have dismissed him from his mind if it hadn't been for Mari's apparent distress. Yet each time he caught her looking over her shoulder, she merely smiled and pretended to be looking at something. She even had gone so far as to point out whatever she had been supposedly interested in. If it kept up he was going to have to talk to her about her fears. Maybe she was under the agency's protection after all and had been afraid she had seen one of her enemies. He was tempted to contact Lucas and ask about Mari to find out if she was a special case. Of course, if she had been put under protection recently, she wouldn't have been allowed to leave the country so soon. All he knew was that he wanted to help her. And if the man turned out to be after him, well, he'd take care of that too.

"Swim or eat?" he asked, watching her slip off the tan cotton shorts and kick them to one side.

Mari tipped her head to one side. "Swim," she decided. "That way we can work up more of an appetite."

Reid had another idea of how to work up an appetite and while he was confident enough he could persuade her, he didn't want their first time to be on a beach. Oh, no, those first hours should be enjoyed in a very comfortable bed.

He flipped two large beach towels out and anchored them with their shoes and the picnic basket then straightened up to peel off his T-shirt. Mari swiftly pulled her shirt over her head.

Reid looked up and his mouth went dry. He, who had always been enamored with thin blondes, thought this curvy brunette was perfection. The strapless bandeau top hugged her small breasts lovingly and the narrow briefs with ties on her lightly curved hips were just right for a man's hands. Actually, every inch of her body was beautiful. Since she had always worn a two-piece suit before today, part of her midriff was pearl white compared to her golden-brown shoulders and legs.

"I—ah—" He cleared his throat. "I hope you brought along some sunscreen or you're going to fry."

Mari looked down at her tummy and wrinkled her nose. "I look like two-tone ice cream."

Reid crossed the sand to stand in front of her. He lowered his head and ran his mouth along her shoulder. "Um, Swiss chocolate," he murmured, then ran his hand over the soft skin of her belly, which contracted sharply at his touch. "And French vanilla. My favorite combination." His mouth slid up to hers as his arms enclosed her in a safe cocoon of warm bare flesh.

Mari's senses immediately set off skyrockets. The more Reid touched her the hungrier she grew for him. She curled her arms around his neck, arching her back so that her breasts thrust shamelessly against him. Her tongue darted past his parted lips and explored the warm musky cavern. She could taste the coffee he had drunk earlier, a taste that left her feeling as giddy as if she had drunk champagne. She felt the pulsing hardness of him and ached to feel him inside her. She moaned softly as memories aroused her as much as his touch did.

Once more! Her body cried out to her brain. *Please, just once more!* But she knew that was impossible if she hoped to keep her cover intact. She cursed the fates for throwing her into such a position.

Reid felt Mari's withdrawal instantly. "I don't want you to be sensible." He groaned, grabbing her hips and rubbing them suggestively against his hard length. "Hell, *I* don't want to be sensible." He rested his forehead against hers. "But I'm getting to the age where I prefer a comfortable bed over

123

sand. Especially for our first time. Although I could be talked into changing my mind if you happened to feel the urge to seduce me. At times I can be incredibly easy."

Mari smiled tentatively. If he only knew it wasn't their first time and there had been one night when they had made love on the sand. Reid had complained because he ended up with sand in the most ridiculous places. And they were in a secluded cove, complete with white sand, green jungle, and blue water. A perfect scene for a seduction. No one would know. Not unless Lucas had someone in one of those trees with a pair of binoculars. Knowing the man, she wouldn't be surprised. She decided she better start talking before she dragged Reid down onto the sand to have her way with him.

"We're both running from something, Reid," she said softly, drawing her finger over the angular planes of his face. And she knew exactly what that something was: the memory of Alicia. She still remembered that first kiss when Reid had called out Alicia's name. "As long as that something haunts us, we can't be together without guilt shadowing that time."

His eyes took on a faraway look. Was he still superimposing Alicia's face over Mari's? But why when the two women were so different? The only similarity he could tell was the way they both aroused him so swiftly. No, he couldn't allow this to happen any longer. Not to one of the sweetest women he had met in a long time. Not when he had finally met someone who allowed him to forget about Alicia. Sure, Mari seemed to have a few hangups, but then so did he. He couldn't condemn her for living with inner fears when he had lived with his own.

Mari knew immediately the direction of Reid's thoughts and she hated herself for causing him pain. She especially hated Lucas for causing them to be in this situation in the first place. She had been so weak then, and it hadn't been difficult for him to bully her into going along with his plan. Mari knew that if Reid ever found out the truth, he'd kill her first, then go after Lucas.

"Didn't you promise me a snorkeling lesson?" she ventured, pasting a bright smile on her face.

The blank look on his face disappeared, replaced by a warm smile.

"That I did." He loped over to the boat and gathered up flippers and face masks. He assisted her with the awkward flippers and kept from laughing as she walked ducklike on the sand for a few moments to get used to them. Directing Mari to stand knee deep in the water, he instructed her in the proper use of the face mask and the tubelike snorkel that protruded upward from the side of the mask.

Mari kept her thoughts to herself as she listened to Reid's instructions. He had her place her mask-covered face in the water and breathe through the mouthpiece. When he felt that she had done that well enough, he showed her how to take a breath of air and dive under the water, reminding her to blow out her excess air gradually and not to inhale.

"You're a natural," Reid complimented after Mari's first foray into the underwater world.

She blushed. "If I'm doing well it's because I have an excellent teacher." She raked her fingers through her hair and laughed aloud her pleasure at the combination of the hot sun overhead, the cool water lapping at her waist, and, especially, the company.

"Let's go again," she begged, grasping his hand and pulling on it.

"Why don't we take time out for lunch? My stomach is strongly suggesting I feed it very soon."

Mari had to admit to a few hunger pangs herself. They put their gear aside and settled on the towels for their picnic lunch provided by the hotel.

"Um, it all looks so good." Mari eyed the cold crab packed in ice, a tasty-looking assortment of fresh fruits and crusty rolls with butter, and fruit tarts for dessert. She was glad mineral water had been included instead of wine. If she didn't keep her wits about her, she might end up in a situation she just might not be able to handle. Keeping secrets from your ex-lover when he has no idea who you are wasn't covered in Spy Tactics 101.

"I thought you wanted to swim more," Reid teased, watching her dig into her share of the crab.

Mari shrugged. "Not after seeing this feast and remembering how long ago breakfast was." She broke off a piece of her roll and held it out to Reid. He leaned forward and covered the tips of her fingers with his open mouth. Keeping his eyes on hers, he plucked the roll from her fingers but didn't draw away. Instead he continued the suckling motion on each of the five digits. He couldn't help but notice how her eyes darkened as she watched him carefully clean each finger. There was something else Reid noticed, an expression in Mari's eyes that didn't fit. It nagged at him because he was certain he had seen that exact expression before, but in eyes that weren't green. He noticed other things too. The short, almost panting breaths, contracted nipples that showed through the wet material of her suit, the way she shifted her legs as if she was uncomfortable in that place he wanted most to bury himself. All of it seemed so familiar, but not with Mari. Reid almost shook his head to clear his thoughts before they drove him crazy.

Mari was having a few crazy thoughts of her own. She felt as if a fist had been slammed into her stomach. Her thumb dropped to caress the rough skin covering his jaw. The warm wet touch of his mouth brought so much to mind—Budapest, dark and gray in the winter, the Balkans in the spring, Berlin's nightlife. All because of a man's mouth making love to her fingers.

"Your—" She paused to pull air into her tortured lungs. "Your crab is getting cold."

Reid smiled. He doubted anything was getting cold around there, much less crab sitting in a bed of ice. If anything, the temperature had risen to an all-time high. He finally took pity on her and released her hand.

"Tell me about your business," he said in a conversational tone totally at odds with the pain he felt in his midsection.

Mari raised dazed eyes. He wanted to talk about her shop when both of them were aroused practically to the point of no return? She grabbed her glass of mineral water and downed it, fervently wishing it was something much stronger.

"I—ah—I own a lingerie boutique," she said finally when she recovered her voice.

Reid cursed silently. Talk about a dangerous subject! The idea of Mari wearing a silk little nothing was very enticing.

"Oh, yes?" He was going to carry on a normal conversation if it killed him!

She nodded, apparently having as much trouble with her voice as he did. "Basically designer lines."

"Meaning expensive."

"Yes."

"I always liked those, what do you call them, teddies?" Reid pondered, picturing Mari in a mauve silk one. "Now that is a sexy item."

Mari thought of the silk men's briefs that she carried and how one particular pair would look on Reid. If she thought about him she might forget the idea of how many women he'd seen wearing teddies in the past few years.

"You seem to have a knowledge of women's lingerie," she said coolly.

He flashed her a wicked grin. "I know what I like." His eyes lingered on the damp bandeau top and what it did to Mari's breasts. If she realized how it looked pasted against her flesh, she would probably pull her shirt over her head and hide the very lovely view from him. He also chanced a quick glance at her legs curved neatly to one side. They were very nice too. "Do you work out?"

Mari blinked. He certainly hadn't lost his touch when it came to throwing someone off base. She had forgotten he was a master at it. But if he changed the subject one more time she might be very tempted to hit him!

"I have Nautilus equipment in my home that I use several times a week," she replied between gritted teeth.

Reid nodded. "Sounds like a nice setup. My apartment building has a weight room but I'm so rarely home I don't get much chance to use it."

Now Mari's eyes swept over Reid's well-toned frame. There wasn't an ounce of fat on his body. Probably running from all those bad guys kept him in shape. Mari remembered the time when she had had to run for her life in spite of the agony that each step caused her. After that she vowed never to run again. She might work out on exercise equipment but she never jogged and she never considered purchasing a treadmill machine.

"What haunts you, Mari?" Reid demanded suddenly, noticing the beginning of horror in her eyes. Just as quickly the expression was masked. "Why is it that I want nothing more than to roll you onto this towel and make love to you, yet I hold back? I know you feel the same way but you always pull back as if afraid." He grabbed hold of her hand. "Were you hurt that badly in the past?" God, that was something he hadn't thought of. Had she been the victim of a brutal lover? Was that why she broke away before things got too hot between them? Was her story about a dead fiancé a sham to keep away prospective lovers?

I am so tired of lies, Mari cried out to herself. *I am tired of having to make up things and be someone I'm not.* Instead she said aloud, "I'm not the kind of person to indulge in a casual holiday affair, Reid. I told you that before." She paused. "I haven't been in the market for a lover and that was by choice. To be honest with you, I *had* toyed with the idea of coming down to Mexico to bask in the sun and find a lover during my stay, but I should have known better. I'm just not the type," she finished on an apologetic note. Even Alicia had never been promiscuous. She had chosen her lovers carefully and could easily count them on the fingers of one hand.

He smiled and leaned over to brush his knuckles along her cheek. "Never apologize for your beliefs. It just goes to show you believe in quality over quantity. There's nothing wrong in that. Hey, I admit I did quite a bit of looking, and sleeping, around years ago until I realized I couldn't remember names and faces." He chuckled. "I even learned that celibacy wasn't so rough."

Mari couldn't help but smile. "We're a fine pair, aren't we? We make ourselves sound like something from the dinosaur era. That's the way we'd be seen, you know."

Reid shrugged. "That's their problem. I guess we're just going to have to deal with this problem one day at a time. If nothing else, we can end up friends."

"I'd like that," she admitted softly, taking the hand he held out and clasping it gently.

Lunch flowed smoother after their talk. Reid teased Mari about her large appetite even as she demurely insisted that she wasn't all *that* hungry. With the conversation now on a more casual basis, they stretched out on their towels for a short rest before going back into the water for another swim before they would have to return to the hotel.

Mari applied sunscreen to her midriff and lay back, closing her eyes against the afternoon sun. She had already noticed that Reid had slipped into a light doze. With his dark skin he would have no worries about burning and since his eyes were closed she could look at him all she wanted. She could look at him with her heart in her eyes and he would never know.

Her body was burning, but not from the sun. Her breasts felt heavy, the center of her femininity melting from dreams of Reid making love to her. With him lying on his back she could visually trace every line of his chest, the whorls of hair down to the band of his briefs that cupped his masculinity in loving detail. It would be so simple to put herself out of her misery. All she had to do was roll over and touch him, look at him with that special expression in her eyes. That would be all it would take. And she would have another memory to store away for those long nights when she was alone again. She sensed Reid would want to see her again after they left Mexico and she knew she would have to discourage him as strongly as possible. As much as she hated to admit it, Lucas was

131

right; once this was started it was difficult to stop, but stop it she would. And she would continue to work hard to keep this situation on her terms. The trouble was, her terms were beginning to sound more and more like Reid's.

Mari was quiet during their last swim. Reid put it down to weariness from the busy day. After he returned the boat to the harbor he walked her back to her room.

"Think you'd feel up to dinner and maybe some dancing this evening?" he asked as they approached her door.

She hesitated. "You know, I'm really very tired and I think I would prefer room service and an early night, if you don't mind?" She watched him take her key out of her hand and insert it in the lock.

He was disappointed, both at missing out on her company that evening and also that she didn't invite him to dine with her, but he was determined not to show it.

"That may not be a bad idea all the way around," he agreed, pushing her door open. His eyes widened and he uttered a foul curse. He pressed his hand against Mari's midriff to keep her behind him. That didn't stop her from seeing the condition of her room.

"My God!" She gasped.

"Stay here," he ordered tersely. He entered the room and made a thorough inspection of the chaos around him. He looked into the bathroom, checked the shower cubicle, looked under the bed and through the closet.

132

Mari could tell, just as she knew Reid could, that the room had been searched and deliberately ransacked. She tried to swallow the bile rising in her throat to no avail. She pushed past Reid and ran for the bathroom.

She hadn't felt this violently ill since her bout with the flu a year ago. She could only kneel on the tile floor and wait until her stomach finished heaving. She could have cried with embarrassment when Reid handed her a glass of water and used a damp cloth to wipe her face. He assisted her to her feet and helped her back into the bedroom and into the chair.

Think fast, Mari! she ordered herself wildly.

"Here." Reid had gone back into the bathroom and returned with two aspirin and another glass of water.

"I guess I should check to see if anything was stolen," Mari whispered, not looking up as she accepted the two tablets with a trembling hand.

"Yeah." He went along with the charade. Surely she couldn't believe that a room would be torn up this way if someone was merely looking for jewelry or other valuables. Something was very wrong here, he could sense it.

Mari would have finished the glass of water just for the sake of having something to do but her hand shook so badly she was afraid of spilling it. She choked back a sob. It was insane. She was worried about spilling water when her room looked like the aftermath of World War III. The bed covers had been torn back, the drawers opened, and clothing scattered haphazardly

133

about. She couldn't help but notice that several pieces of her lingerie had been ripped into small pieces.

"I guess I should call hotel security," she murmured, looking around the room with mixed feelings: horror that someone would come in and do something so despicable and anger that her privacy had been breached. The truth was that she didn't want to call hotel security. If the person in charge was astute they would be able to tell right away that the room had been searched and not broken into with robbery in mind. She could see her watch lying on the dresser next to a pair of diamond stud earrings she had forgotten to put away the night before. Then there was her camera bag sitting on the closet shelf. And she knew Reid had already come to the same conclusion. It was all part of the job they had been trained for. She was just grateful he hadn't asked any questions. As she looked around her body broke out into a cold sweat.

"A thief wouldn't leave a valuable watch and earrings behind," Reid commented casually, too casually.

"Unless we caught him in the act." She knew from the beginning her reason was too feeble. The windows were too narrow to escape from and the sliding glass door leading to the deck was still closed and locked from the inside.

"You don't want to call hotel security, do you?"

She shook her head. "It appears nothing was taken and I honestly don't want questions asked that I can't answer."

"Such as who would do this." Reid squatted down in front of her and took her face between his hands, his thumbs probing the corners of her mouth. "I won't let anyone hurt you, Mari. If you think you know who would do this, tell me, and I'll do whatever I can to help you." He silently pleaded for her help.

Mari's eyes filled with tears. "I don't know." If this was Lucas's way of getting her to leave, she'd personally trash his immaculately kept office. But deep down she feared it was someone from her past who had finally tracked her down. She prayed it was Lucas. That she could deal with.

"I think I'd like to be left alone now," she whispered.

Reid didn't want to do that but he sensed Mari needed time to come to terms with what had happened. His eyes darkened with worry for her.

"You just remember I'm next door. One phone call or even a shout and I'll come running." His thumb wiped away one of the stray tears that had tracked its way down her cheek. He leaned forward and kissed away another tear.

She managed a faint smile and nodded. "I promise."

Although he was uneasy about leaving her alone, Reid left. The moment he reached his room he made a few phone calls. If there were any known enemies in Mexico, he wanted to find out. And if they thought they could strike at him through Mari, they were going to be in for a very painful surprise.

Mari went through the motions of picking up

135

her room. She stuffed all of her lingerie into the wastebasket. What hadn't been destroyed she couldn't have borne to wear anyway. She knew she would have to call Lucas about this, but she wanted to wait until she felt much calmer. He was certain to question her thoroughly and she just wasn't up to it yet.

When the phone rang several minutes later she grabbed at it eagerly in hopes it was Reid.

"Yes, hello."

"Hello, Alicia, I've missed you. Have you missed me?" It was the harsh accented voice from her nightmares.

Mari didn't hesitate. "I'm sorry, but you must have the wrong room. There is no one here by that name." She worked hard to betray nothing more than calm indifference even as she heard a voice that left her screaming inside.

His chuckle sent trickles of fear up and down her spine. "Have I? I apologize." A faint *click* then silence and later a dial tone.

Mari dropped the receiver. This episode hit much too close to home. She hadn't felt very upset at the ruins because she recognized the ploy for what it was—put your object off guard by saying something unexpected. They thought she would break just by someone calling out Alicia's name. She proved them wrong. There was another reason why she hadn't gotten too upset then—the man's voice wasn't the one from her nightmares. If she had heard that voice at the temple, she probably would have sunk to her knees and said anything he wanted her to. She was aware how true her fears were when she realized the dark voice from her past was closer than she ever wanted. The discovery was frightening. She could only sit on the edge of the bed and wrap her arms around her chilled body in a feeble attempt to warm it. She also prayed as she never had before.

She lost no time in calling Lucas, only to learn he was out of his office for the rest of the day and couldn't be reached. Mari wanted to shout at the secretary and tell her that this was a life-or-death situation and demand she contact Lucas. But how could she threaten someone who was only doing her job?

She sat on the edge of the bed, her arms wrapped around her body, and she couldn't remember ever feeling so alone.

Many miles away in another hotel room the man who had called Mari hung up the phone.

"She is excellent at pretending," he told his colleague. "But I know she is Alicia Brookes."

"We still have no proof," the other man told him. "No one has been able to find anything through the office computers."

His smile was confident and very, very cold. "I have proof." He struck his chest with his fist. "In here. That is all I need."

"Shall we terminate her now?"

"No, let her suffer for a little while longer. It won't hurt for her to look over her shoulder for a while and worry when I'll appear."

"What about the man she is with all the time?

We do know he is definitely an agent. The one who used to work with Alicia Brookes."

"If he gets in the way he'll be taken care of. One less for us to worry about is no problem in my eyes." He sat back thinking about the beautiful blond bitch who had acted so high and mighty with him. Of course he had taken care of that as soon as possible. After a while she hadn't been so haughty when she was taken to his interrogation rooms. Perhaps he wouldn't kill her after all. It might be a more interesting proposition to return her to the prison as his personal little pet. This time he would make certain she didn't leave it alive.

CHAPTER SEVEN

Lucas was not pleased with the turn of events and wasted no time in letting Mari know that after she told him about the ransacking of her room.

"You're going to have to get out of there fast," he ordered.

Mari bristled at his imperious tone. "Are you sure you wouldn't prefer I stay here as a damned decoy, so you can catch your man?"

"This is no time to allow your emotions to rule your head, Mari. After all the work I've put into the project I don't intend to see it go down the drain because you've decided to go into one of those female funks."

She rolled her eyes at this. "Fine, here's the deal. I have four days left on my vacation. I'll keep a careful eye out and if you want to send in one of your goons to spy on me, I won't complain. Have a very good day!" she said sarcastically before she slammed the phone down. This time she had allowed her emotions to rule in a most satisfactory way.

For a brief moment Mari wondered if she wouldn't be better off leaving Mexico, but that wouldn't solve anything. If they were even half certain that she was Alicia, the destruction of her room and the telephone call indicated that running would only convince them they were right.

She wondered what Reid was doing. She'd begged off having breakfast with him so she could call Lucas again, for whatever good that had done. When Reid expressed concern for her, she'd told him that she was fine but that she needed to figure out exactly how much of her wardrobe she'd have to replace. He offered instantly to help her spend her money, and she agreed to meet him in an hour and a half.

Mari decided to quit worrying about what would and what would not happen. She had a pretty good idea Lucas would have two agents that Alicia and Reid didn't know on the next plane. She also wouldn't be surprised if Reid had kept an eye on her all night to make sure her intruder didn't return.

Mari looked at the overflowing wastebasket. She had taken most of the clothing that had been thrown on the floor, much of it fouled by splatters of tobacco juice, and pitched it without a second thought. In fact, she thought seriously about sending the bill for her new wardrobe to Lucas!

When Reid first saw Mari he heaved a silent sigh of relief that she appeared calmer than she had the night before. Many times last night he had been tempted to pick up the phone and call her to make sure she was all right, but he respected her need for privacy. After what had happened he knew she would need it, but that didn't stop him from sitting

140

in a chair and staring out the window toward Mari's bungalow all night. He wasn't going to allow her to be bothered again. It also gave him a lot of time to think about why her bungalow had been broken into. It didn't make sense. But then there had been a lot of things that didn't make sense. For the longest time he'd wanted to make love to her, but several things had held him back. One was Mari's vulnerability; something was holding her back just as strongly. And he felt it had nothing to do with a man. He was beginning to wonder about his judgment lately, at least where she was concerned. There was something about her that couldn't easily be explained, and one thing he disliked was puzzles.

"You look positively grumpy," Mari teased, walking up and linking her arm through his. "Did the coffee shop run out of coffee this morning?"

"If I'm grumpy it was because I had to eat breakfast alone." He made all the appropriate grumbling noises.

Mari looked around the lobby, noticing several women who shot Reid interested looks. "I think with a bit of encouragement on your part you wouldn't have had that problem if you didn't want to."

He looked down at her. Something was different; today she seemed more sure of herself, more confident. Now he had something else to wonder about. What brought about this quick change?

"I'm in the mood to spend money," Mari confided, pulling Reid along toward the bank of hotel shops. "And this is probably the best excuse I'm going to have for a long time to buy new clothes."

"What happened to cheer you up?" he demanded, walking along with her.

The prospect of being with you, she wanted to tell him, but said instead, "The enjoyment of buying new clothes lifts any woman's spirits."

Reid chuckled and dropped a quick kiss on the top of her head. "Lady, you're something else. Okay, let's go spend your money."

Mari was pleased to find everything she needed in the many hotel shops. At first she felt a little embarrassed to have Reid along as she chose lingerie, but his matter-of-fact attitude helped dispel that feeling. It wasn't until she noticed Reid picking up a nightgown of rosy silk that her composure faltered. He stood in front of the rack fingering the soft fabric and stared at it with a faraway expression on his face. As if sensing her eyes on him, he looked up and stared at her with the oddest look on his face. Seeing the nightgown, Mari was reminded of her dream.

"I—ah—thought this might be something for you," he said lamely, holding up the exquisite gown.

Mari couldn't have touched the gown if she had wanted to. "The color does nothing for me," she mumbled, turning away hurriedly to indicate to the sales clerk she was finished with her shopping.

Reid picked up the nightgown and held it up as if to overlay it over the back of Mari's body. There was nothing wrong with the color, he wanted to tell her, but something held him back. Maybe it was the memory of Alicia wearing a gown in almost the same color in his dream. Something else nagged at him. That something had to do with Mari. There were times when parts of her just didn't fit. He just wished he knew why.

During the rest of the shopping expedition Mari tried to regain her earlier exuberance, but it just wasn't there and Reid couldn't help but notice.

She did end up purchasing three dresses and several pairs of shorts and tops. Happily she gathered up the charge slips and put them aside to mail to Lucas. She'd tell him this was to make up for the trip to Acapulco.

"How about a late lunch?" Reid suggested as they carried her packages back to her bungalow.

She wrinkled her nose. "If I continue eating the way I've been they'll have to roll me onto the plane. I think I'd just prefer waiting until dinnertime. I'm not really all that hungry anyway."

Reid sobered. He had forgotten Mari would be leaving so soon. And not long after that he would be leaving too. One thing he was grateful for—thanks to Mari, he would be able to leave Alicia's memory behind, except for one tiny part of her he would always carry in his heart.

"Then could I interest you in a walk into town this evening? We could have dinner there. I'll make sure you only have a salad if it will make you feel less guilty."

Mari grimaced. "We don't have to be *that* strict." They skirted the pool area where many of the guests had appropriated lounge chairs to enjoy

143

the sun without worrying about getting sand all over them.

As they circled the concrete walkway Reid's attention was diverted by one of the sun worshippers lounging by the pool. Judging by the man's pale skin he was a recent arrival, but something else about him seemed suspicious. Reid always swore he could smell an agent a hundred miles away, and right now his nose was doing a great deal of twitching. Of course, the man may just be there on his vacation, but Reid doubted it. It was too coincidental that another agent would happen to show up. He'd bet even money Lucas had a hand in this and wouldn't be surprised if he was approached before the day was out.

When they reached Mari's bungalow, Reid immediately took the key out of her hand and inserted it in the door. With a hand held high he silently indicated that she stay behind him. He pushed open the door and gazed over the pristine interior. It didn't look like anything had been disturbed, and his sixth sense said the same thing. Still, he entered ahead of her and checked out the bathroom and closet before he allowed her to come in.

"At least the local wrecking crew decided not to visit me today," Mari said dryly, setting her packages on the bed. She couldn't resist a quick check under the bed but only found a few dust devils.

"Just be glad nothing was broken. Otherwise you would have had to explain to hotel security," Reid told her.

"So I hold wild parties."

He tossed his packages onto the bed and grabbed Mari from behind. "Hey, lady, wanna hold an orgy?" He leered, his tongue snaking out to tickle her ear. She giggled, twisting her head away from his teasing caress. "Okay, how about a plain old-fashioned one-night stand?" He swept her hair away from one ear and planted kisses along the rim. That was when he saw them: thin white scars that can only come from plastic surgery. Reid's hesitation was barely noticeable as he studied the scars before planting slurping kisses along her nape and along to her other ear to examine the skin there. There were thin white lines there also. Something had happened to Mari in the past, something bad enough to cause plastic surgery. Although he wanted to know what it was, he held back from asking her. It was almost as if he were afraid to hear the truth.

"Reid!" Mari laughed, trying to escape his ticklish nibbles.

He stepped back a bit too quickly. She thought the least he could have done was give her a token argument and wondered what caused his retreat.

"How about I stop by at seven and we can walk into the village. There's a few cantinas there that the tourists can visit," he told her, heading for the door.

Mari agreed, knowing she would have enough time to put away all her new clothing and indulge in a leisurely bubble bath instead of having to settle for a quick shower.

Before he left, Reid hauled Mari into his arms and gave her a searing kiss that left her completely breathless. Muttering under his breath, he pushed himself out the door and headed quickly for his own bungalow.

While Mari clipped off price tags and hung up her new clothing, she stopped occasionally to touch her lips. They still tingled from his touch. She ran her tongue over them and could still taste him. If only he were there to reinforce that taste.

Meanwhile Reid was involved in some work of his own. The first thing he did was call Thorson and ask him to do some additional checking regarding Mari Chandler.

"Hey, man, I had a hard enough time getting into her computer file the first time," Thorson told him. "What have you stirred up down there?"

"Not a damn thing," he muttered, wondering why Mari's file wouldn't be as easily accessible as any other one. What was going on? "You're the computer expert, buddy. Can't you break into it without leaving a trace?"

"Is the pope Catholic? Of course I can break into it. It will just take me some time, that's all."

"I want it by late tonight."

Thorson swore under his breath. "Three days."

"Tomorrow morning."

Thorson sighed. "I'll try, but I'm not making any promises. What do you need?"

Reid grinned then sobered. "I want to know if Mari Chandler was in an accident bad enough to warrant plastic surgery. I don't think it was all that recent."

He whistled under his breath. "That's it?" He

expected to hear something much more important.

"That's it."

"Okay, I'll see what I can do." With that, Thorson hung up.

Reid felt a little more relieved that he might find out what kind of accident caused Mari to have plastic surgery. He wanted to find out as much as possible since she hadn't been all that eager to talk about herself. Yet she hadn't asked all that many personal questions about him except for the obvious. He wondered if it was because she already knew everything about him or because her proper Southern upbringing taught her not to ask very many personal questions, even of a man she almost went to bed with. Or maybe she just didn't care. He had a pretty strong hunch it wasn't the latter.

While Reid stood under a hot shower he kept thinking back to Thorson's difficulty in getting into Mari's file. Did that mean she was under the agency's protection? That could account for the plastic surgery. So why didn't the idea feel right to him? He had had to live by his wits and go along with that infamous sixth sense of his for so long that by now it was second nature to him. Something just wasn't right here. The truth of the matter was that he wanted Mari to suddenly break down and confess everything to him. Confess what? That he didn't know either, but whatever it was, whatever trouble she was in, he knew that he wanted to help her in any way he could.

After his shower Reid stretched out on the bed

for a short rest before it was time to pick Mari up. Ordinarily he might have slipped into a light doze, but this time his brain cells were running in high gear and it was all due to Mari. Funny how much he had thought about her during the past week. There had even been a few nights when dreams of her had awakened him. Finally, he did close his eyes and tried hard to concentrate on anything but the occupant of bungalow 12.

Both Mari and Reid were subdued that evening during their short walk to the nearby village. Mari was wondering what had happened to sober Reid in the past few hours and Reid was wondering how to ask Mari about the scars tactfully.

Mari refused to feel despondent for too long and resolved to spend money to make herself feel better. What better way to lift the spirits than to drag out ye old charge cards once more! She stopped by the stalls to look at the wares and ended up purchasing a lacy shawl for herself and one for Denise along with several pieces of silver jewelry that caught her eye. Reid also made a few purchases, a beautiful silver and coral necklace that he explained was for his mother and several hand-painted bowls he planned to put in his living room. Although it would have been nice to corner one of the roving photographers and have their picture taken, Reid made it a rule never to have his picture taken, so he dismissed the idea quickly. In fact, he had been surprised that Mari had never suggested taking his photograph on their outings.

It was as if she already knew he would make up some excuse or come right out and say no.

"I could go for a double margarita right about now," Mari announced, tucking her packages into the large straw bag she carried.

"That's all you want?"

"Well, whatever else they can find to feed me wouldn't hurt. I'm not a very good drunk," she confessed.

"Get sick, huh?" he asked sympathetically.

Mari shook her head. "No, not really, I just don't feel as if I'm in control. Actually, it's only hard liquor that does it to me. I can drink wine without any problem." She'd only had that problem since her hospital stay. She wasn't sure if it had been due to all the drugs she'd had to take then or just another new quirk of Mari's. Alicia had always been able to drink anyone under the table, except Reid.

Mari did have her double margarita along with a delicious fish stew and warm corn tortillas to mop up the spicy broth. What surprised her was that Reid sat across from her drinking straight tequila. She watched him lick the salt off the back of his hand, suck a slice of lime then down the potent alcohol. He ate most of his stew, downed several more drinks, and still remained relatively sober although there was a dark glitter in his eyes that hadn't been there before. And during the whole meal he watched her every move the way a cat watches a mouse.

"I wish you'd stop that," she muttered, staring back at him with as much anger as she could muster. She knew that he wanted her even more than

149

he had over the past few days. Her body tightened in reaction.

"Stop what?" He lounged in the chair, one arm flung carelessly across the back. He looked as if he was thoroughly enjoying the idea that he was making her uncomfortable.

"I know what you're trying to do, Reid, and I'm not going to allow you to ruin my evening," she informed him in a properly frosty tone.

He smiled, a very dangerous smile that sent tremors skittering up her spine. "I thought I was acting very much the gentleman."

"Obviously our definitions differ," she muttered, taking a healthy sip of her drink. She was tempted to ask the waitress for another but decided not to take the chance. She didn't relish the thought of spending the rest of the evening in a fuzzy world, especially when she was with a human shark who looked ready to pounce on his prey at any moment.

After dinner, Reid suggested they check out some of the local cantinas and walked into the first one they passed. They weren't there five minutes when he regretted his idea. Mari may not have been beautiful in the traditional sense but there was something about her that attracted a man's attention; after all, she'd certainly attracted his. Wearing a deep-purple silk dress that flirted around her knees, she created a male fantasy. He was convinced that every man there wanted to find out what was beneath her dress. He grumbled that there wasn't a table available and practically shoved her out of the cantina.

"What is wrong with you?" Mari demanded, stunned by his action. Before she could say any more he headed down an alley and pulled her behind him.

First he made sure they were alone, then he leaned back against the wall even as his mouth covered hers and his tongue plunged roughly into her mouth. Settling himself against the wall, he pulled her intimately against his body. Through the thin silk of her dress she felt him growing hard but it didn't set off any of the alarms it had before. Moving her hips with his hands, he rubbed her back and forth against him. His mouth absorbed her throaty moans and he pressed down harder.

Instead of growing limp in his embrace, she found herself breathing hard as if she had run a long and arduous race. With every thrust of Reid's tongue she felt his energy flow into her body. She wrapped her arms around his shoulders and gave as passionately as she received. For long moments they were lost in a world of their own making as they kissed as if there was no tomorrow. Their mouths mated in the way their bodies demanded to. Reid tasted Mari again and again because he couldn't get enough of her; Mari did the same because she desired all the memories she could get. That was when she made her decision. There would be no more holding back, no more cold showers. This would be the night they would make love.

"Reid." She panted, pulling her mouth away only to have it captured again as his hand brushed over her breast and found the peaking nipple. It

151

ached with sensual delight as he rubbed it between his fingers. Little did she know that he wasn't about to give her a chance to have second thoughts. She finally succeeded in putting a little distance between them. "If we stay here any longer we're going to wind up getting arrested."

"I don't care as long as they put us in the same cell," he muttered hoarsely, deciding that nothing tasted as good as Mari's mouth. "Do you realize what a sexy mouth you have? If I was any good at poems I would write one about it."

She laughed shakily, stepping back and placing her hands lightly on his shoulders. "Why don't we go back to the hotel where we can be more comfortable?" She stared into his eyes so he would receive the full import of her meaning.

"Are you sure? Because if you back away from me this time I'll probably go crazy."

Mari cupped his face with her hands and leaned forward to brush a light kiss across his lips then slowed to pull his lower lip into her mouth. She heard him groan with delight at her action.

"As sure as I can ever be," she replied softly. At the moment she felt her body humming from his kisses. Now she wanted it to sing a full aria. "Reid, I want you to make love to me."

Reid drew in a deep breath. "Honey, that is exactly what I plan to do."

During the walk back to the hotel, Reid kept a close hold on Mari with his arm draped over her shoulders while she circled an arm around his waist. In days to come, neither would remember what exactly had been said, but it didn't matter because their bodies and hearts would always remember that magical moment.

Reid wasn't sure exactly why he stopped by the front desk on their way to his bungalow, but he cursed himself for doing so for weeks afterward. There he found a telephone message from Thorson insisting he call him back as soon as possible, no matter how late it was.

"I have to make a long-distance call back to the States. It's important that I call back right away," he explained, folding the paper and placing it in his shirt pocket. "Why don't you go back to your place and I'll over as soon as I can." He was beginning to hate his suspicious nature that insisted he find out what his friend had to say before it was too late.

"All right." Mari managed a brief smile that didn't mask her disappointment. At her door, Reid kissed her thoroughly and left after muttering a few curses about the invention of the telephone.

Mari worried about what the telephone call was about. She doubted he would have bothered returning anyone's call at such a time except for Lucas's. Was Lucas going to insist he leave Mexico right away? Was he going to be sent back to Europe? Her stomach clenched with each wild thought that ran through her brain. The trouble was, none of them were all that wild. After all, she still remembered what it had been like over there. She remembered a lot of things. She stopped in surprise after she opened the door and found an envelope with the hotel crest in one corner pushed under the door and her name written on the outside.

"What?" she breathed, grasping the card. Her eyes widened when she realized that it wasn't from Reid.

We miss you, darling Alicia. Please come back soon so we can continue our little games.

There was no signature. And there didn't need to be. There was no question as to who had sent the note.

Strangled sounds escaped from her throat as she grasped the envelope and prepared to throw it away. Deciding she didn't want the offending note anywhere in her room, she slipped out of the bungalow and ran down to the beach to throw it as far into the ocean as possible. When she returned to her room she sank onto the bed and concentrated on stopping her trembling. She knew she had to get herself in hand before Reid came back or he'd have no trouble telling that something was drastically wrong.

Reid put in his call the moment he reached his bungalow. His stomach rolled as he thought why Thorson wanted him to call him back right away. He had already forgotten that he had demanded to know immediately what his friend had learned.

"This better be good," Reid grumbled when Thorson's sleepy voice answered the phone.

"Good?" Thorson groaned. "This time you owe me one whopping big favor. The rest of Mari Chandler's file was hidden so deep it was next to

154

impossible to find and damn near impossible for me to erase my tracks. If Lucas ever finds out what I did, both of our asses will be in a sling because I won't take the fall alone."

Reid felt cold. That happened when they kept someone very important under their protection. Had she been a vital witness from a tricky case and was now hiding out? If so, whose side had she been on in the beginning? "And?"

"There was no indication the lady was in any kind of accident or any reason for her to have plastic surgery."

"The protection program," Reid murmured. "It's got to be."

"Yeah, I agree with you, although we haven't had that many women and I always had access to the other files before without any difficulty. Like I told you before, her background is a little too perfect." Thorson yawned. "Watch your back, friend."

His piece of advice was the last thing Reid wanted to hear. That meant Thorson felt Mari couldn't be trusted. At the moment Reid knew he couldn't face her without demanding answers to questions she wouldn't be allowed to answer, if Thorson's hunch was right.

"Okay, thanks," he said finally. "I really appreciate what you did and the risks you took."

"Believe me, you're going to pay for this favor in spades," Thorson told him. "Now if you don't mind I think I'd like to get a few more hours sleep before it's time to get up and go to the barn"—his personal description for the obscure building the agency was housed in.

"Yeah." Reid hung up and stared at the phone for a full ten minutes before he was able to pick it up. He dialed Mari's room number and waited through several rings before she answered.

"Hey, I'm sorry about this, but I'm going to have to wait for them to call me back," he lied without a qualm. "I forgot about the time change and assumed the person I needed to talk to would be in the office now. Luckily, someone was there and I left a message. It wouldn't be right to have them ring your room."

"I understand." Reid was so lost in his own blue funk that he didn't hear the quaver in Mari's voice. "It certainly isn't your fault." She couldn't resist asking, "Will I see you tomorrow?"

"For breakfast." In fact, if he had everything in perspective in time he'd just appear over there in time to serve her breakfast in bed . . . in his own special way. With luck, they might not leave until dinnertime. "I'm sorry, Mari. I'll see you tomorrow."

Mari understood but that didn't stop her from assuming the worst. Lucas had called him and given him the special code indicating there was an assignment coming up and Reid was to return to D.C. right away. He'd be working alone, anything could happen. Especially if Black Death decided to go after him instead of her. Her imagination ran riot as she got ready for bed and lay under the covers staring at the bathroom where the slightly closed door filtered the light coming from the small room. It seemed fitting that it began to rain just as she fell asleep.

Too many memories of the past crowded Mari's brain and ended up disturbing her sleep in the most distressing way. She tossed and turned under the covers as the harsh voices invaded her dreams.

"Just tell us what you know, Alicia." The voice was silky smooth, but oh so deadly. "You don't owe them anything. Do you see anyone trying to rescue you?"

"I don't know anything. I keep telling you that." The cultured British accent sounded cold and condescending. She closed her eyes to shut out the pain radiating throughout her body. When she'd heard from one of the other prisoners that this man was a master of pain, she hadn't had any idea what exactly that meant until she was face to face with him. Alicia was blessed with a special gift; she could read and memorize facts and figures in a matter of minutes and by using self-hypnosis she could bury those facts until they were required. But the pain her captor inflicted on her took away any memory of what she had found out before she had been arrested. Whatever information the coldly handsome man had wanted was gone forever.

"No, no, don't hurt me. I know nothing. Leave me alone." Mari moaned, tossing her head from side to side. Her hands clenched the covers as she tried to force herself to awaken. But as in the past, it didn't happen. She would just have to suffer through the rest of the nightmare. Her scream was caught in her throat when she sat up straight, her eyes dilated with fear, her body slick with sweat. At first, she started to pick up the phone to call Reid. She didn't care it was after three in the morning; she needed him to hold her, she wanted him to banish her fears by making love to her. Luckily, she had second thoughts and slowly replaced the phone before she completed her call. Overhead she could hear the rain pouring down and the wind blowing wildly around the bungalow. She was surprised it hadn't awakened her earlier.

Mari buried her face in her hands. This dream was even more potent. She couldn't seem to stop shaking. Probably because of the events of the past few days and the note she'd received that evening, not to mention her fear that Reid was going overseas again.

With all that was going on, she knew she would have to face Lucas again. It was time to find a new safe place. Time for a new name and past to learn. She'd have to leave everything behind again. At least, it wouldn't hurt as much as it had before. If this continued for years she would become an old hand at changing identities.

Refusing to stay cooped up in her room with her nightmare hovering overhead like a dark cloud, she pushed the covers aside and jumped out of bed. No matter how bad it was outside, the howling elements were better than anything she faced inside.

Not bothering with a robe, Mari stepped out onto the deck. She righted a chair that had overturned in the wind and tipped her face back to feel the cleansing rain. By breathing deeply and clearing her mind she was able to calm herself. Looking up at the dark and angry sky, she only wished Reid was beside her to appreciate the wildness around them.

Reid wasn't sure what woke him up. It couldn't have been the bad weather, he'd slept through much worse. He got out of bed and padded into the bathroom to splash some cold water on his face. No matter how he'd felt, he should have gone over to Mari's bungalow, even if it was only to talk. Being so abrupt with her had been cruel, but he hadn't known what else to do.

When he left the bathroom he stopped by the window to draw the drapes aside and look out. He could see a light burning in the bathroom of Mari's bungalow, but what caught his attention was the ethereal figure standing on the deck in a flimsy nightgown. Her body looked open, inviting the storm. He wanted that same primitive passion directed toward him.

Without thinking twice, Reid pulled on a pair of jeans, left his room, and crossed the brick path to the other bungalow. As if she sensed his presence, Mari turned at the exact second he reached the end of the deck. Her hair was plastered against her head, her nightgown clinging to her body like a second skin, her eyes were bright with the excitement of the storm. She had never looked more beautiful.

Words weren't needed as Reid crossed the few remaining steps to the waiting Mari. He pulled her into his arms and covered her mouth with his.

They were wet and cold from the rain but they needed no other warmth than each other. Mari clasped his head with her hands, running her fingers through the wet strands of his hair, moving her mouth back and forth under his.

"Make me forget," she uttered an aching plea, rotating her hips against him and feeling the masculine bulge against her belly. "Don't leave me alone again. Please, give me tonight."

Reid didn't bother to figure out what she meant. All he knew was that the woman he desired was in his arms. He swept her up into his arms and would have walked into her room but her hand pressed against his bare chest stopped him.

"Your bed," she insisted quietly. "I want to feel more than just your body around me. I want to feel your spirit in the room possessing mine the same time your body possesses mine. I need that right now."

He didn't question her reason, he merely carried her across the way to his room, slid open the door, and carried her inside.

CHAPTER EIGHT

Reid gently laid Mari onto the bed and stepped back. How many other women could be soaking wet and still look beautiful? he asked himself.

She smiled up at him and proceeded to peel her nightgown from her body with the most seductive movements he had ever seen. At the same time Reid was trying to get rid of a pair of wet jeans that refused to part with his body. Still smiling, Mari moved over to the edge of the bed and assisted him with his disrobing.

"You smell like the rain," she whispered, pressing her cheek against his abdomen, her hand slithering downward over taut skin. "And wind and fire." At the last word her fingers curled lovingly around his hot pulsing shaft.

Reid closed his eyes and drew in deep breaths to keep from exploding at her gentle touch. There was so much he wanted to tell her: how beautiful she was, how good she smelled and, especially, how good she felt to him. Not to mention how special she was to him. He hadn't realized how dead to the world around him he'd been until he had met her. She was alternately shy and sensual around him, keeping him off balance. No matter how much she frustrated him he couldn't just write her off.

He combed his fingers through her hair, pushing it away from her face. "And you smell like woman," he murmured before his mouth lowered to cover hers in a kiss that transcended all time. In fact, it was as if they had all the time in the world. He stretched them out on their sides, their bodies touching lightly. His mouth rolled over hers in a gentle motion that encouraged her lips to part. This time she took the initiative by sliding her tongue along his lower lip and then slipped inside to explore his dark smoky flavor while she silently urged his hand to cover her breast. Smiling into her eyes, he rubbed his thumb over the nipple before lowering his head to take it into his mouth. Mari moaned, feeling the motion spiral downward to her womb. She writhed under his touch and rotated her hips under his exploring hand. One finger, then two, probed the moist depths, withdrew and probed again in a movement guaranteed to drive her crazy.

Mari raised her arms, combing her fingers through the damp hair curling on his chest. Her fingernails lightly scratched the brown nipples that sprang to vibrant life under her touch. She then tipped her head forward to tongue one nipple to further life before tasting the other. She decided that Reid not only smelled like the elements, he tasted like them too.

Mari felt very greedy—she wanted it all, and she began by nibbling around his collarbone, then ran her tongue over his whisker-rough chin before moving up to his ear. Reid smiled and began a new assault on Mari's body. His hands tightened on her hips before moving around to cup her softly rounded buttocks as he pulled her up hard against his aroused body. He positioned her so she would feel the full urgency of his desire and rubbed himself against the aching juncture between her legs. His mouth covered hers, his lips hard, warm, and urgent.

Then he kissed her again. This kiss was slow and lazy and hot, his tongue looking for all the places where her mouth might be hiding the candy he craved.

Mari arched up, silently inviting Reid to possess her, but he wasn't going to take her up on her invitation just yet. He wanted to have her just as wild for him as he already felt for her.

Sexy words were whispered in the dark as their hands traveled over curves and planes of bare skin. To Reid, Mari appeared a known yet also an unknown factor. It was as if she sensed his movements before he did. Her mouth trailed over his bare chest, her tongue catching the salty taste of him. She throbbed for him, ached for him. Reid, as a lover, was all that she remembered, and more.

Soon, all time for exploration was over. Reid rolled Mari over onto her back and rolled on top of her, bracing his elbows on the bed on either side of her. For long silent moments they looked at each other, memorizing features, adjusting to the new position. With a heavy groan he bent his head to take her lips again. This time his passion was unleashed another notch. He thrust harder, demanded more, and left Mari panting, clinging to his shoulders, every nerve in body alive and clamoring for more. Mari smiled and lifted her hips until she touched him. It was enough to send Reid over the edge. He groaned and plunged deep into her. That was when he froze. He was stunned how familiar she felt to him. It was as if they had been lovers in another lifetime. For one split instant their eyes caught, their souls merging as strongly as their bodies.

He knows! Mari thought hysterically even as her hips moved in a never-forgotten rhythm. This was all too familiar for both of them.

Who is she? Reid asked himself, even as he thrust deeper and deeper into her moistness. *Why do I feel as if I'm replaying an important part of my life? Why do I feel as if I'm making love with Alicia?* In that split second he saw the look of terror in her eyes. How many more secrets were there between them? Then it became all too clear. He should have known! Damn it, he should have known from the beginning, but everything was so different! Everything but the body. Oh, no, the body could never lie. No other woman's body felt like Alicia's. No other woman responded to him the way she had. The way this woman was responding to him right now. His mind whirled with questions, but his body was rapidly overriding any chance of halting even as his brain continued working on overdrive.

No, the body couldn't lie, but his memories just might be a little bit cloudy after so many years.

164

After all, he had been haunted by Alicia for more than three years, why wouldn't he believe the first woman he cared for was a reincarnation of her? For the first time in his life Reid was so confused he didn't know what to believe. Nothing made sense any more. All he knew was that the woman beneath him was more than enough to make him lose his soul and he wouldn't regret it.

Mari couldn't keep from looking into Reid's questioning eyes, but she couldn't have stopped either. It was too important for their bodies to have the reunion they had craved for years.

Mari ran her hands over his perspiration-slick shoulders. She had never forgotten all this, but memories just weren't the same as the real thing. She wrapped her legs around his hips to keep him as close to her as possible. Pretty soon, the heat throbbing so insistently within her blossomed outward. Her muscles tightened, her breasts swelled until they felt painful, and the lava flowing through her veins intensified to a fever pitch. Judging from the tight cast of Reid's features, he was falling into the same cavern. Their bodies moved faster and faster until Reid groaned and collapsed. He rolled to one side to relieve Mari of his weight but kept an arm around her waist. He turned his head to look at her.

There was so much he wanted to ask her. Nothing made sense any more. He only hoped Mari could shed light on the confusion he was experiencing.

Mari smiled mistily up at him and fell into a light sleep the same time Reid did.

He woke her twice during the night. The first time he took her with an almost primitive simplicity, rousing her from sleep to basic, aching need in a matter of minutes, then fulfilling her in a fashion that was as dominating as it was devastatingly satisfying. The second time was leisurely, as he took great care with her. He wooed and seduced her as if she was a virgin all over again.

When Mari next woke dawn was just breaking and Reid slept heavily beside her. She lay under the covers staring up at the ceiling, her eyes scratchy and swollen from unshed tears. She couldn't afford to face him when he awoke. She slipped out of bed carefully, hesitating every few seconds to ensure that Reid didn't wake up. She pulled her nightgown on over her head and crept out of the room as silently as she could. As soon as she reached the outside, she ran to her bungalow and locked herself inside, as if locks would keep Reid out if he woke up too soon and guessed where she was before she had a chance to leave the hotel. Mari showered and dressed quickly then tossed her clothes into her suitcases. When she finished she picked up the phone and dialed the front desk.

"Yes, this is bungalow twelve." She spoke in a tightly controlled voice. "I would appreciate if a bellboy could be here right away. I'm checking out."

She kept herself under strict control, knowing that now was not the time for tears. She had the rest of her life for those.

* * *

The moment Reid woke up he knew he was alone in the room. Still, he called out Mari's name, only to be greeted by silence. He bolted out of bed and checked the bathroom before pulling on a pair of shorts and running across to her bungalow. The door was locked, but that didn't stop him. He jimmied the lock and entered the room. The bed was made up and the room seemed empty. No clothes hung in the closet, no cosmetics littered the bathroom counter. There was nothing to indicate that the room had ever been inhabited.

Reid returned to his own room and dialed the front desk only to learn that Ms. Chandler had checked out earlier that morning. With that piece of information rolling around in his head, he sat on the bed and thought about everything that happened that night. Every curse known to man fell from his lips. He wished he hadn't fallen asleep when he should have forged ahead and cleared up the questions rolling around in his head. He should have found out everything he could. But there were other ways of finding out what he needed to know. Reid wasn't the agency's best operative for nothing. He packed his clothing and checked out of the hotel, arriving at the airport just in time to catch the next plane to the States. Mari Chandler wasn't going to escape him that easily.

There was no chance of Mari escaping Reid even if she had wanted to. Memories of their night together would haunt her for the rest of her life. The day she discovered that she would not bear

Reid's child as a result of their night together, she huddled in bed all morning and cried. She called Denise at the shop and told her she had a cold. Her croaky voice added credence to her lie. She wanted to do nothing more than stay home and wallow in her misery.

Since there had been no lovers in Mari's life since Reid she hadn't bothered using any kind of birth control. Deep down she knew that having his child without his knowledge would have been very wrong, but she would have still gone ahead. After all, he and Alicia had talked many times of having children, and it wouldn't be right to deny him. All she could do now was go on the way she had before—living one day at a time.

In an effort to do just that, she called Lucas and demanded a new identity.

"I have already anticipated your request and am working on something for you," he informed her in his no-nonsense voice. "You will be given the particulars when they are available and not until then."

"And when will that be, the year 2000?" she asked sarcastically, gripping the receiver with nerveless fingers. "I have to get away, Lucas. Those goons could show up on my doorstep at any moment."

"You'll be taken care of," he soothed. "I already have some men on the case. So in the meantime, just proceed with your life as usual. Nothing is going to happen to you."

So why didn't Mari feel as safe as she should?

Probably because the person she truly feared finding her wasn't part of any terrorist group.

"Mari." Denise approached her hesitantly a few days later, her face creased with concern. "Is there anything wrong? What I mean is, you went away to rest and relax and you come back looking worse than when you left. I hope you didn't drink the water." She made a feeble joke.

Mari managed a tiny smile. "Everything is fine, Denise. I think I'm still suffering from jet lag. Besides, you know what they say: You always need a vacation to recover from the vacation you already took."

But Denise wasn't that easily convinced. She knew that Mari skipped lunch more often than not and she doubted her boss was eating very much at home. Mari's weight dropped at such an alarming rate that Denise insisted she see a doctor. Mari merely smiled and told her she had planned on losing a few pounds after all the eating she did on her trip. To back up her story she shopped for new clothes, saying she wanted a new image.

But Denise wasn't easily appeased. No matter what she claimed, Mari wasn't the same woman who had left for Mexico several weeks ago. She didn't appear interested in anything, although she always used to take personal care to check out each shipment. Now she spent more time in the back of the shop, working on the books and arranging to open a new store in Charleston. She even made several trips there over the next month to find the right property and interview prospective employees. Denise had turned down

169

Mari's offer of the manager's position, explaining she didn't feel she was management material. Besides, she preferred staying in Charlotte and working with Mari. But if Mari couldn't find someone to take over the shop right away, Denise would handle it until Mari hired someone. Mari used that as an excuse to work even harder looking for someone to take over the new shop. It was important to keep herself so busy that she was too exhausted to do any more than sleep at night. But it didn't help. Reid haunted her dreams the moment she lay her head on her pillow.

Something else haunted Mari—the idea of Reid coming after her. When he didn't appear on her doorstep during the first week, she convinced herself that he received an assignment from Lucas and was now out of the country. She had spoken to Lucas only once since her return to see if he'd heard anything about her tormentor in Mexico. She refused to ask about Reid and she was surprised that her former superior hadn't mentioned him.

Finally Mari convinced herself that she was getting her life back on the proper track. She began sleeping better and ate more than the few nibbles she had before, although her weight didn't increase by an ounce. She blamed Alicia's metabolism for that although she knew it could also be nerves. When she put her makeup on each morning she'd see a different woman in the mirror. She began using a few brighter colored eyeshadows and dressed less conservatively than before.

She wondered if the two personalities were finally blending into one. Mari had been the complete opposite of Alicia from the very beginning, so it was only natural that after a while they might decide to get together. Mari couldn't remain a coward for the rest of her life. She had been hiding much too long, afraid to take any chances. Until she ran into Reid. With him she took the biggest chance of them all. And even though she had to leave him in the end, she didn't feel she had lost everything. She still had those hours imprinted in her heart.

"You've changed, Mari," Lucas said the moment she said hello into the telephone that rang late one night.

"The prospect of another birthday in a few months will do that to a woman," she said dryly. "And to what do I owe the honor of this call?" *Please, God, let Reid be all right. I couldn't handle it if he were hurt or . . .*

"I thought you would like to know that we found the man who broke into your room in Mexico."

"Who hired him?" Mari demanded, although she felt she already knew. The tingling at the base of her neck gave her her answer.

"He hasn't talked but when we mention Black Death to him he gets very uncomfortable, so we'll assume he did the hiring." Lucas paused. "It would certainly help us out if you would remember the facts from that time you were there."

Mari could feel her body break out into a cold

sweat. "How long ago was this phone line checked?"

"Several moments before I called you." He acted affronted that she would presume he would be so careless. His voice grew cold. "We need to know, Mari."

She wiped her hand over her face. "I remember nothing, Lucas and I doubt it will ever come back. Even Dr. Jackson told you that part of my memory might stay hidden forever."

"Alicia never had a problem giving me the information."

Unwilling to talk to him further, she slammed the phone down and then took it off the hook to ensure that Lucas couldn't call her back.

Alicia never had a problem giving me the information.

That was true. Alicia had virtually a photographic memory and by using self-hypnosis could bury information in her subconscious, bringing it back when she was debriefed at the end of each assignment. Few people knew of her talent, and only Lucas knew the key words to trigger Alicia's memory. Except the last time he tried them they didn't work. By shutting off what she had known as Alicia, Mari was safe. Lucas was angry that she couldn't give him the vital information. It took the intervention of the agency's psychiatrist for Lucas to finally leave her alone to work things out in her own way. Usually he was a patient man, but this time his patience had reached its limit. Naturally, the terrorists would have changed codes and meeting places, but any little bit would help in subduing one of the most violent groups in the world.

Unable to sleep after the trauma of Lucas's phone call, Mari went upstairs to work out until she exhausted herself. When she finally fell asleep, she was still tormented by nightmares of Alicia's time in prison. In the morning, when she finally dragged herself out of bed, her face was pale and violet shadows circled her eyes.

"Now this I have to have," Denise announced holding a red lace bustier in front of her. "Rod would love it!"

"Rod? What happened to Sean?" Mari questioned.

Denise grimaced. "Mari, where have you been the past few weeks? Sean and I split up ten days ago after I found him cuddling up to a very sexy blonde in his apartment."

"Blondes have more fun," Mari murmured wryly, counting out boxes of sheer stockings and checking them off against the invoice. "And I suppose you're also going to take that horribly expensive Christian Dior nightgown too? I don't know how you manage to live with the small fortune you spend here."

"Thank heavens for employee discounts." She laughed. "Mari, do you realize you and I would probably make the best-dressed list for lingerie?"

"Too bad we see it more than anyone else," Mari returned. "Especially with the prices listed for some of these next-to-nothing pieces of lace."

Denise's face lit up. "You *are* getting better! That's the first joke you've made in a long time."

Mari smiled. She doubted it was a sign she was feeling more like her old self, but it did feel good to smile and enjoy life again.

"When do you plan to open the Charleston store?"

"Six weeks from Saturday." Mari set the invoice down. "Lorraine called me this morning and said the carpeting was installed without a hitch. The drapes are going to be hung today. I thought I'd drive down there this weekend and take a look. I also have to find the time to work on the ads announcing the grand opening."

"And you wondered why I say I'm not management material. If anyone should know my true self you should know how lazy I really am."

Mari smiled. If anyone *wasn't* lazy, it was Denise with her never-ending energy. The young woman was usually in the shop well before opening time and long after closing. While she insisted she didn't like to supervise, she unwittingly kept a close eye on their part-time clerk who worked afternoons and Saturdays. Mari doubted she could survive without Denise's unfailing good humor permeating the shop and her life.

Their work was interrupted by the chiming of the bell over the door announcing a visitor. Denise went out front and returned with a long white box.

"Hmm, who's the admirer?" she teased, handing Mari the box. "A box this long has to hold roses."

At first she didn't want to take it, fearing they might be from Reid. If they were she couldn't handle reading his name on the card. She shrugged, acting as nonchalant as possible as she set the box on her desk, pulled the pink ribbon off, and lifted the top.

"Oh, my God," Denise breathed, her eyes wide with shock.

Mari was just as stunned. Instead of spring blooms or roses as she expected, the box was filled with dead flowers. With trembling fingers she picked up the card nestled among the gray and black stalks.

Remember the many hours we spent together?

"Who would do something so sick?" Denise asked, gesturing to the box.

"I don't know," Mari lied, wanting to scream out her rage. Was this to be her fate, being followed for the rest of her life the way a mouse runs from a vigilant cat? She would have to call Lucas as soon as possible. She also wanted to cry. In the beginning she may have dreaded that the flowers had come from Reid, but she had also hoped that they had.

Reid couldn't stop thinking about Mari. Actually, he was thinking about the woman who claimed to be Mari Chandler. He started out in the town where she was reported to have attended college and spent hours looking up old school records and trying to track down old friends. The more he saw, or didn't see, the more Reid was convinced that Mari wasn't who she claimed to be. At night he lay alone in his hotel room remembering the night of the storm and all that Mari had given him during those beautiful hours. The more he thought about it, the more he was convinced of Mari's true identity. Was that why she looked at him with fear in her eyes? But what was the reason? She had no reason to feel afraid of him. He'd be the last person to hurt her. If anything, he would do everything in his power to protect her. He knew there was a great deal more to the story and he was tempted to fly to D.C. and confront Lucas, but he knew the bastard only too well. If he didn't want to talk he wouldn't. The last time Reid had talked to Thorson the other man informed him that Lucas was furious at Reid's disappearance. He ordered that anyone who heard from Reid had to report his whereabouts to him or else. Reid told Thorson to forget receiving his call, he'd take care of Lucas in his own time. Oh, yes, he'd take care of him, but good, if his suspicions turned out to be true. He decided it wouldn't hurt to return to the college tomorrow and see what else he could charm out of the clerk, who had slipped him her phone number this afternoon, before he moved on. His next stop would be Charlotte. It appeared that was where he would receive the answers he required.

Mari was furious. Of course, when it came to Lucas, that was nothing unusual. Why wasn't he doing as he had promised and having someone tail her? Why wasn't he taking her out of Charlotte so she could begin her new life? Why the hell couldn't he take better care of her? The more she thought about it, the angrier she grew until she felt she couldn't think straight.

She went through the first and second floor of her house pulling all the drapes shut. She couldn't look out to see if anyone was there, but no one could look in either.

Although Mari was furious with Lucas, she was also frightened at what could happen to her if a certain man wasn't found very soon. She knew this time she would be killed or worse. The sadist in charge of the prison also ruled the terrorist group. He wasn't happy unless he was inflicting pain.

With Alicia he had done even more. He had turned her into a human mass of whimpering fear. He had broken the strong woman's spirit and enjoyed watching her cower from him every time he had her brought into his rooms. That he never tried anything sexual with her wasn't surprising as far as he was concerned. He found creating pain much more exhilarating than making love with a beautiful woman. There had even been rumors that he was impotent.

Mari poured herself a stiff drink and downed it in one gulp then poured herself another. She never thought of getting drunk as being much fun, but after the day she'd had it sounded like an excellent idea.

Denise was quiet during work the next day and shot Mari speculative looks. As soon as the shop was empty for more than five minutes, she cornered her boss in her office.

"Something's going on here that I don't understand," she said without preamble. "Perhaps I'm better off not knowing, but I do want you to know that if there is anything I can do to help I'm here."

Mari's eyes filled with tears. She reached out and hugged the other woman.

"Thank you," she whispered. "I only wish that you could help."

Denise smiled. "Next time I suggest you take a vacation just order me to take inventory, okay?" It was her most hated chore.

"You gotta deal."

The bell over the door chimed.

"So help me, if it's the florist delivery boy again I'm going to throw him out," Denise said, walking out of the storeroom.

"Go get 'em, tiger." Mari laughed, grateful she could laugh again. Maybe things weren't so bad after all. Sure, and penguins could fly.

Denise returned a few moments later with the strangest look on her face. Mari panicked instantly and gauged how quickly she could get out the back door.

"I only have one thing to say," Denise said quietly, her eyes glittering with undisguised awe. "If you don't want him, can I have him?"

Movement by the doorway caught Mari's attention. The tall man standing there was something out of a dream, or maybe a nightmare. She gripped the nearby shelf before her knees gave out.

"Hello, Mari." Reid's voice was devoid of emotion, which signified danger.

It took all of her willpower to remain standing. The last thing she wanted to do in front of this man was faint.

CHAPTER NINE

Reid stood there drinking in the sight of her. Damn, she was beautiful! She had grown very thin, her angular curves accented by the slim sapphire skirt and matching blouse. Her black belt had a gold inverted V design on the front. This was not the woman he remembered, the one who dressed conservatively in quiet colors. He sensed that this new image was a very recent change and that her weight loss just might not be due to a diet.

Mari was still speechless. She saw the lambent fire in his eyes as he leisurely swept her from head to toe.

"Denise, this is Reid Morgan," she said in a low voice. "Reid, Denise Conroy, my assistant."

"We've already met, so to speak." When he turned to the other woman all traces of anger had disappeared from his manner. "I hope you don't mind if I steal your boss away for the rest of the day. We have some catching up to do."

Denise's eyes lit up. To her horror, Mari could see that Denise thought Reid was the reason for Mari's blue mood and would be only too happy to help a budding romance along.

"No problem," Denise assured him. "You two just run along. I'll lock up."

Mari turned on Reid. "I have work to do," she said through gritted teeth.

Denise's eyes widened at her boss's anger. "All the new stock is already checked in, Mari. I'll put everything away this afternoon after Sara comes in." What she really meant was for Mari not to let this one get away!

Reid walked forward and took Mari's arm in a viselike grip. His feral smile told her that he knew very well that he was the last person she wanted to be with. But that wasn't going to stop him from getting her alone.

How had he found her? She hadn't told him the name of her shop or even what town, much less the state, she lived in. She should have known that if he wanted to find her badly enough nothing could stop him. She had thought that when he woke up alone he would have grown angry at her and written her off as too much trouble to go after. Too bad he hadn't.

"I'll just get my purse," she said quietly.

Reid nodded but didn't release her arm as Mari led the way to her office. Once inside, he walked over to the file cabinet and looked around as she opened her desk drawer and retrieved her purse.

They remained silent as they walked outside. Mari headed for her Toyota, but Reid steered her toward a dark sedan with a rental sticker in the window.

"How did you find me?" She didn't speak until they had been driving for almost twenty minutes.

181

"You should know I always find what I want."

Mari turned her head to look out the window because she couldn't bear to look at Reid. His cold voice and manner dropped the temperature in the car by about twenty degrees. Oh, yes, he had always been an excellent tracker.

You should know I always find what I want.

Did that mean he knew who she was? Or was he just playing with her? A mirthless smile touched her lips. Perhaps he thought she worked for the other side. Now there was a laugh; too bad she didn't feel very much like laughing.

"I've been on the road constantly for quite a while now." Reid spoke up. "Is there a place near here that serves decent food? As much as I'd like to see where you live, I doubt you'd invite me for a home-cooked meal."

She ignored what could have been either a soft jeer or wistful longing in his tone. "Turn right at the next light and then a left turn two lights down. There's a restaurant that serves very good barbecued food." Then she could have bitten her tongue; barbecued food was Reid's favorite. At least, it used to be.

He shot her a telling glance and made the proper turns. On the outside, the restaurant was nothing spectacular to look at, but Reid had learned long ago not to look at exteriors. He should have looked past that mild-mannered exterior when he first suspected something was wrong with Mari. When she had left the hotel without a word for him, he could have cheerfully strangled her. And over the past few weeks, during all the miles he had flown and driven, he still wanted to strangle her. Then he saw her in that stockroom standing there with the look of shock and pain, yes, that was it, pain in her face and his desire to curve his hands around her throat disappeared. All he wanted to do was haul her into his arms, pull her down to the floor, and make love to her. He wanted to find out if that night in Mexico had been his imagination or not. He felt as grim as he probably looked. It wasn't fair that she looked so beautiful when he felt like the back end of an old dog.

Reid requested a booth near the rear of the restaurant. He slid into the seat across from Mari instead of sitting beside her as she had expected him to do.

"Damn you for looking so beautiful," he snarled, staring at her with hot eyes.

She glared at him. "If you'd like I can go into the ladies room and take off my makeup and show you the dark shadows under my eyes and my pasty skin. It took me the better part of an hour this morning to hide the damaging evidence."

He stared at her bright blouse. "Quite a switch from the soft colors you wore in Mexico. You put on a very convincing act." He may have wanted to make love to her but he also wanted to hurt her for putting him through hell, and he was doing an excellent job of it.

Mari vowed to call Lucas the first thing when she got home and demand that he drag Reid back to Washington. Lucas! He had two of his men watching her, they could be outside right now. She glanced furtively around the restaurant but couldn't see anyone who fit the bill. Someone might even be calling Lucas right now, she hoped.

"I always buy a new wardrobe each season," she informed him coldly. "It was time for a change."

"Hm, I wonder if I had anything to do with it."

"Don't make me laugh."

They paused when the waitress approached them for their order. Both ordered the sampler plate since it was the first item on the menu and neither wanted to admit they hadn't looked at it yet.

"Why did you run away from Mexico?" Reid demanded.

"I told you I had to leave soon, that my vacation was almost over," she countered.

"You had two days left." He had intended they spend them in bed so he could confirm why her body and responses were so familiar to him and settle the question that had been nagging him since that first time they had made love.

She forced herself to look him in the eye. "I chose to leave when I did for reasons of my own."

"What reasons?" he clipped.

"None of your business."

Reid's eyes narrowed. In the past hour Mari had showed more spirit than he had seen the entire time in Mexico. Oh, it wasn't that she could be considered mousey, but she always seemed to want to blend into the background and give in instead of offering her own opinion. Well, she certainly wasn't blending into the background or giving in to him now!

Mari looked down at her hands that lay

clenched in her lap. "Reid, we had a very nice time in Mexico, but there were no promises made on either side," she began softly, gearing herself for the hardest speech she would ever make—because it was all a lie. "And now I'm back where I belong and you should be back where you belong."

"Basically, you're saying we indulged in nothing more than a one-night stand," he stated bluntly. "That's the way you see us. Lady, you should be in Hollywood; you're a great actress. Now, how about the truth, for a change?"

She whitened under his attack but refused to back down. "I *am* telling the truth. Don't condemn me for seeing things the way I do. I have a life here and you're not in it."

"Then why do you admit you look like hell under that careful application of makeup?" Now he reverted to sarcasm.

"My work has been very hectic lately, and, contrary to what my assistant said, I do have a great deal of work waiting for me. I'm in the process of opening another shop in Charleston, and it takes all my time to get everything done before the grand opening," she said blithely. "I'll catch up on my sleep when it's over."

Reid noticed that during their conversation Mari had taken her napkin and unknowingly ripped it to shreds. She wasn't feeling as cold and indifferent as she claimed.

When their food arrived Mari looked at it blankly as if she had no idea how it got there. She had no appetite but forced herself to pick at the spicy slices of beef, pork, and ham. When Reid offered her a piece of cornbread, she shook her head.

"You were right, this place has great food," Reid told her, deciding to hold off on any more verbal attacks until they were alone. He wasn't going to tempt fate by upsetting her further in case she broke down. For a while he was positive she would have gladly spit nails at him. He'd like to see her that way again. He had an idea if she really got going he'd be guaranteed quite a show of fireworks.

"Would you like coffee?" Reid asked after they had finished their meal.

Mari shook her head. "I'd just like to be driven back to my shop so I can finish my job. I hope by now you realize what a mistake it was for you to come here." Her manner was decidedly chilly.

Reid grinned. "Oh, no, my sweet lady, you're not getting rid of me that easily." He looked at the check, dropped several bills on the table, and escorted Mari out of the restaurant. When they were settled in the car again he turned toward her. "Now do I get an invitation to your house?"

There was no hesitation. "No."

Reid watched her facial expressions. There was a trace of fear in her eyes. For some reason she didn't want him to know where she lived. It looked like he was going to have to do this all on his own. He switched on the engine and drove out of the parking lot. It took Mari several minutes to realize he was driving in the direction of her house.

"Where are you going?" She was bordering on panic. Why couldn't he have just stayed out of her life and left her with her memories? If he stayed much longer, she was sure he would guess her identity soon—if he hadn't already.

"Just sit back and relax."

Mari's address and telephone number were unlisted, but she knew that Reid had sources most people didn't have. She prayed Lucas's goons were waiting in front of her house. *They* could haul Reid back to D.C.! Then she could sit down and have that good long cry she was entitled to.

Since Mari refused to direct Reid, he had to refer to a street map a few times but eventually he found her house. He pulled into the driveway and got out, looking around with amazement.

The three-story brick house with dark-red trim looked warm and inviting to a man who hadn't had a real home since childhood.

"No wonder so many cleaning ladies say they don't do windows," he muttered, looking up to the third floor with its many windows. Not to mention the large green lawn in the front and the carefully tended rose bushes bordering the house. For the first time in days he thought about Alicia. She would have hated this—a house that indicates permanence and all that went with it. But Mari was the kind of woman a man automatically equated with home and hearth.

Mari's hands shook violently as she inserted the key into the lock. She knew she could talk herself blue in the face, but Reid was still going to enter the house with her whether she wanted him there or not.

"Now I suppose you expect me to offer you coffee or a drink?" she asked caustically, placing her purse on an elegant mahogany table in the entryway.

"What I want from you I doubt you'd offer just now."

She drew in a deep breath from his blunt statement. She spun around, her hands clenched at her side. "Why are you doing this?"

"Damned if I know." For the first time she could see the strain in his features. He must have worked very hard to hide his weariness for as long as he had. He raked his fingers through his hair and sighed. "Maybe because you make me see beauty in a world I was always convinced was going to hell in a handbasket. I haven't felt very sociable for a couple years now. Mexico was my first vacation in that same amount of time. You also helped me to forget about the woman whose death I caused." His face was lined with furrows of pain that couldn't be healed by medicine.

Mari's eyes widened at this revelation. "What?" she asked hoarsely.

Reid cursed silently. He let too much out. Without saying a damn word, she encouraged him to talk, when he should keep his big mouth shut. But maybe this would turn out to be in his favor. He'd just watch her facial expressions to see if she would give herself away. "We used to work together." He was going to have to edit this very carefully or he'd end up revealing more than he should. "When I told our boss we were getting married he wasn't too happy, so he sent me off to one place and her to another. Because of problems there she died. We would have been better off just getting married and resigning then and there. Instead, she's dead and it's all my fault."

Mari placed her hand flat against her stomach. She'd had no idea that Reid might have felt guilt over Alicia being sent to the Middle East. If anything, Alicia should have just refused to take the assignment. She wished she hadn't heard his confession because there was nothing she could do to absolve him of a guilt that had been gnawing away at him for years. She still sensed he had an inkling she wasn't who she said she was and if she hoped to keep her secret, she was going to have to get Reid out of her home as soon as possible. She walked over to him and laid her hand on his arm, feeling the taut muscles jump under her touch.

"Did you ever stop to think that she could have turned the assignment down?" she asked quietly. "You can't blame yourself for something that was beyond your control."

He hauled her into his arms and held on to her so tightly she feared her ribs would crack. "How can someone so lovely be so wise?" he whispered hoarsely. Why did he want to read something else in what she said? Was he hoping for too much when there might not be anything there?

"Because I've lived with pain and sorrow too." Mari buried her face against the slightly rough skin of his neck, feeling the rapid tattoo of his pulse beneath her lips. "You can spend the rest of your life pining over 'what ifs' but it won't make them go away. Especially when they weren't your doing to begin with." She closed her eyes in shared pain. By all rights she should calm Reid down and send him on his way. She should do everything in her power, including coldblooded lying, to get him out of her life once and for all. But it was difficult when she stood there in his arms, feeling his strength around her and inhaling the rich scent of his after-shave combined with his own unique scent. It felt so cruel to push him away when all she wanted to do was take him by the hand and lead him up to her bed.

How long they stood there in each other's arms didn't matter. Shadows outside deepened until the entryway was almost dark save for a nightlight burning at one end that came on when the room turned dark. All they cared about was drawing upon each other's strength, and when they finally pulled away each felt bereft.

"I—ah—I guess I should take you on a tour of my house." Mari spoke hesitantly, still cognizant of the deep emotions welling up inside of her. She didn't want him to go just yet no matter what her practical side said.

"I'd like that." Reid heaved a silent sigh of relief. He'd been afraid she would ask him to leave, and this reprieve was welcome.

Mari led him through a comfortable-looking living room dominated by an off-white sofa facing a large fireplace. Accent shades of mint green and pale gray lent an illusion of warmth coupled with cool. A painting of a cloud-shrouded waterfall hanging over the fireplace added to the feeling.

The kitchen had the same color theme although it was a brighter gray and a cheerful yellow, which spilled over into the dining room that held a polished oak table and tapestry-covered chairs.

Upstairs Reid saw the study where Mari worked on her paperwork so she didn't have to spend her evenings at the boutique. The guest room was decorated in red and gray, done in such a way that the combination didn't jar the senses but flowed around the visitor like a soft wrap.

Then there was Mari's room. Here the colors were peach and gray. The queen-size bed was covered with a quilt with a swirling pattern of the two colors. A small pearl-gray velvet love seat with peach decorator pillows sat in one corner next to a tiny bookcase filled with books. Her perfume permeated the air. The atmosphere was almost sterile, and he'd bet his last dollar that no man had ever entered this room before. He looked at Mari who stood near the doorway, her hands clasped tightly in front of her.

"Shall we look at the next floor?" she asked nervously.

Reid appeared surprised. "The attic?"

She shook her head, a ghost of a smile touching her lips. "You'll see soon enough."

He certainly did.

"I'm impressed." Reid walked around the exercise room noting and touching each piece of equipment.

"Actually, I'm very lazy," Mari confessed.

He swept his hand over the contents of the room. "This doesn't look like the kind of a place a lazy woman goes to."

"Wanna bet? I couldn't even imagine getting up early to go jogging. If I want to work out at two in the morning, I can." She didn't want to explain the real reason why she worked out so diligently.

Reid walked over to the spa in one corner. "I'm surprised you were able to have this up here, judging from the age of this house."

"It belonged to the previous owner. He'd had all the floors reinforced for this room and their waterbed. His wife had injured her back in a car accident so it was part of her therapy."

Reid thought of relaxing naked with Mari among the jets of water. The idea of making love to her there was very exciting. All it would take would be some convincing on his part. He noticed her staring at the spa as if she'd never seen one before. Hm, maybe it wouldn't take very much after all.

Just take it slow and easy, he advised himself, walking over to where she stood. Don't blow it or you just might find yourself out in the cold. It wasn't until he stood beside her and murmured her name that she looked up with a glazed expression in her eyes. He had no idea what she had been thinking of.

Mari was remembering almost four years ago when Alicia and Reid were on assignment at an elite spa in Switzerland. There had been bubbling hot springs a short distance from the hotel and they had stolen away to the bubbling pool late one night. She doubted anyone could have spent more passionate hours than they had that night. Mari opened her mouth, ready to say something about it. In her blindness to the moment she almost revealed her secret, but Reid caught her attention by moving his mouth over hers.

His mouth was hot and searching when it covered hers. After weeks of frustration searching for the real Mari Chandler, he was determined to lose himself in her body. He was going to brand her as his until she knew it as well as she knew her own name.

Mari was past protesting. When Reid's mouth slanted over hers, her lips parted automatically, accepting the rough intrusion of his tongue. She curled her arms around his shoulders to ensure that he wouldn't leave her. Her brain may have been screaming how wrong this was but her body was saying just the opposite. She craved Reid, craved him the way she used to crave cream buns and opera creams as a child. No, she wanted Reid even more. Giving up chocolates and cream buns had been much easier than giving up Reid would be. She was greedy, just as greedy as she had been in Mexico. For some reason the fates were giving them another chance to be together, and she wasn't going to allow it to slip through her fingers. She relaxed her body, melting against him.

That was when Reid knew he had won. He drew her more fully into his embrace and widened his stance so her pelvis was cradled tightly against his.

"I should beat you for putting me through hell these past weeks," he breathed, threading his fingers through her hair. His mouth punctuated each word with love nips along the graceful column of her throat.

Mari lowered one of her hands to press lightly against the front of his slacks where his pulsing warmth radiated outward to her caressing palm. "Do you still want to beat me?" she murmured, looking at him through slitted eyes. Her mouth was swollen and moist from his kisses, and her nipples blatantly peaked through the soft fabric of her blouse. She never looked more desirable. She had no idea the two personalities were finally blending into one—Mari's warm beauty had combined with Alicia's inherent sensuality. Reid never had a chance.

His hands still tangled in her hair, he dragged her head back and administered long, drugging kisses until Mari felt boneless in his arms. He lowered his head to take one pouting nipple into his mouth through her blouse and suckle, taking the dusty-rose pebble between his teeth. Mari moaned and begged him not to stop. When Reid finished loving one, he moved to the other until they stood erect, the aching flesh sensitized to the damp fabric covering them. Then Reid's hand slipped between Mari's legs, rubbing gently over the fine wool. Feeling her heat sear his palm and her hips move against his hand was almost his undoing. With great haste he pulled her blouse out of the waistband of her skirt and unbuttoned it, allowing it to drop to the dark-gray carpet. The tiny lace confection some people might call a bra left him breathless. But when he slid away her belt and skirt and found wispy panties and a lace garter belt holding up sapphire silky hose, he almost exploded.

"Where're the controls for this?" he asked hoarsely, gesturing toward the spa.

Mari stepped to one side to lift the top of a nearby box and flipped a switch. Immediately the jets flowed into action. She watched Reid divest himself of his clothing and remove the rest of hers before assisting her into the warm swirling water. It didn't take him long to realize that the bottom was slightly slanted so that he could set Mari on the bench in front of one of the water jets and stand in front of her.

He grasped her wrists and pulled them around his neck before delving his fingers into her femininity. He wasn't surprised to find her moist and ready for him. His eyes were looking directly into hers as he thrust deeply into her.

Mari gasped at the rightness of it. She wound her legs around his hips and met every thrust with a seductive movement of her own. Mouths and tongues mated as intimately as their bodies did.

"I want to be so deep inside you you'll never forget me," he said roughly.

"I couldn't forget you if I tried."

"You're mine."

"Yes."

"Do you like this?" He rotated his hips, leaving her moaning her pleasure.

She wanted to scream out loud but could only whimper "Yes."

"Touch me. Show me what I'm doing to you."

As their bodies moved from one plane to another, Mari ran her hands over Reid's body in another attempt to memorize every muscular swell and hollow. This time she didn't think about this being the last time they'd be together; she knew it had to be. But soon all she knew was the intense heat beginning where their bodies were joined and spiraling outward. Her veins were rivers of molten lava, her skin felt as if it would go up in flames any moment. She didn't think she could take much more without shattering into the universe.

Reid's thoughts must have closely echoed hers because he soon thrust faster and deeper until he collapsed, spilling himself inside her. Mari closed her eyes and held onto him tightly, wanting it to last as long as possible. She felt drained and renewed all at the same time.

"Think we should try it in your bed next time?" Reid murmured in her ear.

Mari was too exhausted to reply. She had been living on pure nerves the past few weeks, and Reid's lovemaking had released all the tension from her body, leaving her feeling replete. In fact, she was so relaxed she could have easily fallen asleep in the pulsating water. It was Reid who finally roused her out of the warm water and wrapped her in one of the rose-color oversize towels that sat on a nearby wicker stand before carrying her downstairs to her bedroom. There he proceeded to make leisurely love to her until she begged him to fully possess her. Afterward, Mari fell into the deepest sleep she'd known for a long time.

For Reid, sleep wasn't as easy. There were still too many questions unanswered.

Who was the real Mari Chandler? Nothing he'd seen made sense, and he figured the only way he'd learn the truth was to ask her outright.

He glanced down at the woman sleeping so peacefully in his arms. He carefully disengaged her limp form from his embrace and slipped out of bed. After arranging the covers over her naked body, Reid slipped into the bathroom for a quick shower. Assuaging his curiosity, he unashamedly explored her cabinets and medicine chest. He was surprised to find no form of birth control. It did force him to stop and wonder if she had been protected tonight or the last time. The thought of her bearing his child put a lump in his throat, but he couldn't afford to think about that now.

When he finished in the bathroom, he crept down the hall to Mari's office, where he switched on the desk lamp and closed the door behind him.

Mari's files were kept in perfect order in an oak cabinet that was incredibly easy to break into. They told Reid all he wanted to know about her business. Naughty but Nice had shown a profit in a little over nine months and her plans for her second shop were neatly drawn up, complete with estimated sales projections and notes on her new manager and clerks.

Another drawer revealed her personal files: birth certificate, school and medical records, household ledgers, but nothing that would help

197

him. Reid didn't stop there. He methodically checked each file in hopes of finding something, anything.

Mari thrashed wildly in the wide bed. Reid's arrival had sent her unconscious fears upward into her recurring dream.

"You're a very lovely woman, Alicia." The deep, heavily accented voice could be as painful as the lash of a whip or as soft as silk. *"I'd hate to see that beauty destroyed."*

"Of course you would hate it." Alicia's boarding-school accent didn't falter under the pain she felt. *"Just the way I'd hate to see you killed."*

"Never play games with me, Alicia. You'll only lose."

"No-o-o." Mari moaned, her fingers digging into the sheets.

Just like so many times before, her eyes flew open and shifted to the right for the reassuring sight of the night-light that sat on her dresser. Except tonight there was no warm yellow-orange glow. For the first time in over three years Mari had gone to bed without a light and woke up to complete darkness. She panicked and suddenly reverted back to Alicia, who had spent so many hours in a pitch-black cell. She sat up in bed and screamed—screamed as she had never screamed before.

Reid's head snapped up at the first scream. By the time the second one rent the air he sprinted down the hall to the bedroom.

When he reached the bedroom the bed was empty.

"Mari? Where are you? Are you all right?"

He would have searched the rest of the house for her if he hadn't heard a faint whimpering sound from the bathroom. Reid walked in and found a sight that left him speechless.

Mari, her eyes wild and features paper white, huddled in a corner between the commode and bathtub. When she saw a dark shadow standing in the doorway she pressed her knuckles against her mouth.

"Can't do what you say. Know nothing." She whimpered, but it appeared she was talking more to herself. She had no idea Reid stood there; in her tortured mind she saw another tall man with darker skin and handsomely savage features. A man who delighted in creating pain in others. "Dark here. Rats. They hurt."

A cold wave washed over Reid. If he hadn't stood there and heard her cries, he wouldn't have believed it.

Sweet, Southern belle Mari spoke with Alicia's crisp British accent.

He thought of the horror books he used to read, of one life taking over another. But that only happened in books! This was reality!

Mari held out a trembling hand in front of her unseeing eyes. She was so caught up in the past she had no idea where she was. She mumbled words that made no sense to anyone but her.

Reid could take no more. He strode into the small room and gathered her up into his arms.

"No!" She screamed, fighting him with all her might. He dodged her flailing arms and carried her into the bedroom where he wrapped her struggling form in a sheet and pulled her back into his arms.

Reid couldn't be sure if it was minutes or hours before Mari finally calmed down. During that time he listened to her whispered pleas not to be hurt and speeches she must have made to herself when she was alone and, most especially, he learned of the man called Black Death who alternately wooed and hurt Alicia. And the more he heard the more he wanted to know. His mind seethed with an inner torment that was nothing close to what this woman had felt. He had been told Alicia was dead. Lucas stood there and calmly told him she had died in that damn medical center.

By now Mari spoke only soft disjointed phrases that made no sense. A very somber Reid rested his cheek against the top of her head, his fingers smoothing the damp tangled waves from her fevered brow. Hot tears filled his eyes and for the first time in more than three years, Reid wept tears of anguish for the woman he had once loved and lost and for the terror-filled woman he now held in his arms.

CHAPTER TEN

It was late morning when Mari next awoke. When she tried to turn her head she winced from a pounding headache. With the advent of morning also came the realization that Reid probably knew most of the truth. She remembered little of the previous night except her intense fear of a man standing over her, a man she knew would hurt her. A man she expected to hurt her. Except there was no pain this time. Instead he had wrapped her in a sheet and carried her to bed to soothe her nightmares away with the gentle touch of his hand and voice. She also recalled salty droplets caressing her face, tears that weren't hers, before she had fallen asleep in arms that held her tightly, the same arms now holding her just as securely.

"I see you've finally decided to join the land of the living." The body next to her shifted his weight.

She knew she couldn't hide from him forever, but a few days' reprieve so she would have a chance to get her thoughts collected wouldn't have hurt.

Mari didn't know what to say, but she didn't

need to worry. Reid had already moved away and sat up on the edge of the bed. The grim expression on his face and lines of strain around his mouth and eyes didn't make her feel any better. It was obvious he was furious.

"What happened to Alicia?"

Reid's coldly voiced question flicked across her like a whip.

Mari slowly got out of bed and walked across the room to her closet. Once she had her robe belted tightly around her waist she felt ready to answer.

"Alicia Brookes died three years ago from injuries sustained in the line of duty," she replied quietly, forcing her eyes to meet his frozen gaze.

Reid thought of his earlier search of Mari's bedroom. All he found were mainly conservative clothing in quiet colors and while her lingerie was of excellent quality, it wouldn't have been described as sexy. He could remember the little bits of nothing Alicia used to wear. Not to mention the times she had worn nothing at all, explaining underwear would ruin the lines of her outfit, and Reid would go slowly insane waiting until he had her alone.

"I want to know what the hell is going on here," he grated, his face filled with grim determination. "And who you are."

"You already know who I am."

Reid uttered a vile curse. "Quit waltzing around the truth before I decide to take this place apart piece by piece." The heaviness in his gut told him he might not like what he'd hear, but he had to know.

Mari knew this was no idle threat. Reid was furious enough to create as much damage as was physically possible, although she knew he would never hurt her.

"There's nothing to tell."

"Bull."

She drew upon all her reserves of inner strength to remain calm. "I'm going downstairs to fix some coffee. I suggest you be dressed and out of my house before I come back for my shower." With that she left the room with as much cool dignity as she could conjure up.

Reid showered and dressed, but he had no intention of leaving until he received some answers.

Mari stood at the counter and watched the coffee drip into the glass pot as her mind spun with questions.

Why did she have to have the nightmare last night when Reid was there? Why couldn't she have had the sense to switch on the night-light? Why did she have to freak out in front of him and reveal God knows what? Why had she given in to him again when she knew better? Why, why, why? She buried her face in her hands, silently entreating the taunting voices to leave her alone.

"I'm not leaving here until you tell me what's going on." Reid's voice sounded behind her. He spun her around and thrust his hands into her hair, tilting back her head to an almost painful angle. His sharp eyes searched every inch of her face looking for something, anything to give him a clue. When he reached her eyes he found it. By looking closely he could see a green disk floating in her eyes. "What color are your eyes, Mari?" he asked softly.

She tensed. "Green."

"You wear contact lenses."

"So do a lot of people. They're very handy when you're nearsighted and can't see more than ten feet in front of you." Alicia had twenty-twenty vision.

Reid narrowed his eyes. So she was going to continue lying to him. What he had to do was find the right buttons to push.

"Perhaps this is the wrong time to ask, but are you protected?" He used his soft dangerous voice again. "I didn't see anything in your medicine cabinet and I admit I was a bit too overheated to think of it these past few times."

Mari froze. She had been safe the last time, but now she was close to the wrong time of month. Reid read her answer in her face.

"So the lady doesn't fool around all that much," he mused with a cold smile on his lips.

"I should have stuck with my pristine record," she retorted. "I would have been much better off."

Reid's fingers ran lightly over her face and around to her ears. No matter how much Mari fought it she couldn't help the shiver of desire rippling through her body and he didn't miss her reaction. He smiled, a thin smile that was fraught with a cold darkness Mari hadn't experienced in years.

"When did you have plastic surgery?" His fingers ran lightly over the narrow scars behind her ears.

Mari stiffened. It had been so long she had forgotten about the scars. Most men wouldn't have noticed them, but Reid wasn't most men.

"What did you look like before?" he asked idly, fingering the silky strands curling around her ear. "In fact, I haven't seen any pictures of you around here. I'm curious as to what you looked like before." He was growing angrier by the moment and was determined to take his fury out on her. "I bet your hair used to be more blond, didn't it? And your eyes aren't really green, are they? Then there's your weight loss since I last saw you. I'd say you've always been much thinner. Oh, I can imagine you used to be the life of the party and not the shy little thing I met in Mexico, right?"

Mari tried to put her hands over her ears to shut out his relentless voice, but he gripped her wrists and held them firmly to her sides.

"No!" she shouted, closing her eyes. If she couldn't shut him out one way, she'd try it another. "You're trying to upset me and I don't like it. Now I want you out of here in ten seconds or I'm going to call the police and have them throw you out."

"Damn you, tell me about Alicia!" he yelled back, holding her wrists so tightly there were sure to be bruises. "I'm not leaving until you tell me what happened, Mari, so talk!"

"I can't!" she screamed, feeling the tears course down her cheeks. "There's nothing to say so leave me the bloody hell alone!"

Reid released her and stepped back. He'd noticed her choice of words, can't and not won't. He also hadn't missed her using a British slang word.

He looked at her closely. It didn't take an expert to see the strain she was feeling. Her face was as pale as a sheet of paper and her eyes were dark and shadowed. Alicia never backed down from a fight; she always gave as good as she got. This woman was ready to fold at any second. When Mari didn't answer right away, Reid steered her toward the round ice-cream table in one corner of the kitchen and sat her down before going back to pour two cups of coffee and setting one cup in front of her.

"Why did they tell me you were dead?"

Mari rested her forehead on the heel of her hand. She wanted nothing more than to drink the bracing brew before her but her hand was trembling and she didn't want Reid to see how upset she was.

"Please don't ask any questions, Reid," she begged.

"Lucas is behind this, isn't he? Damn it, Mari— or is it Alicia—this wouldn't be your idea. You wouldn't play such a cruel joke on me. Not after all we shared."

Tears slipped down her face and dropped onto the table. "I'm not the same person any more, Reid," she whispered. "Can't we just leave it at that and you go your way and leave me to mine? I'm sure you'll forget all about me once you're back to your work."

"I haven't forgotten about you during the past

three years. Why would I do it now when it appears I've found you again?" he demanded tautly.

"Because it's better for the both of us if you do."

"Is it?"

Mari forced herself to drink some of her coffee for courage and then had to force her eyes to lift to look at Reid. What she saw took her breath away. He looked the part of a tortured man except this wasn't playacting. Pain and suffering bracketed his features and he looked ten years older than his thirty-eight years. He reached across the table and took her hand, lifting it to his lips.

"There are things you're not supposed to tell me," he guessed. "And I bet Lucas is behind that too, but we never kept secrets from each other. Please, don't do this to me. I need to know what is going on, what happened."

Mari shrugged. Perhaps it was better if she told him the truth. If she could persuade Reid there was great danger in his staying with her, he just might understand and get out before it was too late.

"I swore to Lucas that I wouldn't tell anyone what happened," she murmured, rubbing her thumb over the back of his hand. She needed the touch of his skin to give her reassurance. "It was part of the deal I struck with him."

Reid squeezed her hand in a silent reply. He felt the cold entering his blood, a warning that he would hear something he wouldn't like.

Mari collected her thoughts, unsure where to begin. She had finally made the decision to tell him everything, but she wasn't sure she could go through with it. Not in one sitting. There was too much pain involved.

"I—ah—I know there's a lot to tell you, but please don't ask for all of it now," she pleaded, a catch in her voice. "I'll tell you enough to ease your mind for now but that's all. Let me warn you, it could also make it worse."

Reid bowed his head, positive silence was best. He could feel her hand trembling beneath his touch. What was so painful to her that she found it difficult to talk about it?

Mari wet her lips. "One thing about the Middle East, it's very hot and there are areas that are very dirty, and you know how Alicia hated filth." She chewed on a fingernail. "Alicia was there barely a week before her cover was blown. She was arrested in the middle of the night; she wasn't even allowed to pack or put on other clothing. She was very distressed that she had to go to jail in her nightgown. The terrorist group she was to find out about owned that part of the country and their leader was in charge of the prison. She never learned his real name. He preferred to be called Black Death."

Reid inhaled sharply. Every good agent knew of the man; he was known to have no conscience and created pain wherever he went. His termination would be an excellent thing. And she had been a prisoner of that bastard!

Mari turned her head, looking out the window, but she didn't see the green lawn with its border of roses. She saw a tiny cell with an even tinier window and the dirt and rats around her.

"You know, what they say about Black Death is nothing compared to the real man," she whispered. She swallowed, hoping to relieve her dry throat. It was harder to talk about it than she thought it would be. "He enjoyed inflicting pain. One day Alicia watched him break a man's legs just because his coffee arrived late. As for Alicia, he —ah—he broke her cheekbones because he said she was too haughty for her own good. He also threw her into a cell with twenty men so they could knock her down to size, if you understand my meaning."

Reid's hands clenched into fists. He couldn't keep back the vile curses dropping from his lips at the idea of what had happened to her in that cell.

"Reid, they didn't hurt her," she assured him quickly, grasping his hand. "The men were political prisoners and for some reason, they didn't even try to rape her. One man explained that they understood why she was put in there and they wouldn't give Black Death the joy of knowing he had turned them into animals. Unfortunately, because they didn't go along with his plans, several of them were executed as an example to the rest." Her eyes grew bleak. "Then she was put in a cell by herself. Sometimes she was left alone for days and she prayed her death would be swift. Alicia was certain she had been forgotten and would die there. When she was positive that that would be her fate, a guard would appear and take her to the interrogation room for 'questioning.'" Mari halted, unsure she could go on.

He sensed her agitation and knew it was time

for a change of subject. Or at least something she could handle. "How did you get out?"

Mari smiled, but it didn't reach her eyes. "The rebels blew up part of the prison and broke their people out. Alicia got out at the same time. She wouldn't have been able to make it if it hadn't been for some of the other prisoners carrying her out. She was so weak from lack of food she could barely walk and she also suffered from several broken bones." She added wryly, "She wasn't a very pretty sight. I doubt you would have recognized her. By sheer luck she was able to get word to Lucas and he had her flown back to the States."

"Why did he tell me you were dead?" Reid demanded.

Mari shook her head. "She didn't know he had done that until months later. He explained in the beginning they weren't sure she was going to live and they didn't want to raise any false hopes." And because Lucas had other plans for her, she thought to herself.

"But I should have been there with you," he ground out, thinking up ways to punish his superior. "He wouldn't even let me see you. I had barely arrived at the medical center when he had told me you were dead. I went to England for your funeral! I comforted your parents! Did you have to let them suffer too?"

Mari flinched at the raw anger in his voice. "Alicia had no choice," she retorted. "Lucas said that Black Death was convinced she hadn't died and that the only way to keep the story straight was to take on a new identity. There was another reason."

"Don't tell me, you decided you preferred being a shopkeeper."

She shook her head at his sarcasm. Needing time to regroup her thoughts, she stood up and walked over to the coffeemaker to warm her coffee. She held up the pot in silent question but Reid shook his head. His system was humming along just fine without the need of any caffeine.

"Lucas said she had to drop out of sight because Black Death was still after her," she explained when she returned to the table. "There was also the chance he would go after her family and you if he had the barest hint that she was alive. That way he could ensure she would come out of hiding."

"Why does he want you so badly?" *Why did she talk about Alicia as if she didn't even exist?*

"Because he's convinced she carries in her head the names and locations of all his agents. He's probably changed them over the years but that hasn't stopped him from wanting to punish her for getting them in the first place. The man has no conscience, Reid. She escaped and for that he will make her pay very dearly, if he finds that she's still alive," she said fervently.

"But Lucas would have the information also," he argued. "Surely you gave it to him as soon as you were well enough."

She told him it hadn't happened that way. "The doctor said it was all the trauma she had gone through. Possessing the information caused very painful headaches so the best way to fight it was to forget all about it."

"And the new face?" He had to know everything. The hell with holding back. He had been hurting for over three years. The fact that Alicia/Mari may have also been hurting all that time was immaterial. Right now he was selfish enough to care only for himself.

"Alicia was a mess, Reid," she said baldly. "What they performed on her was reconstructive surgery. I gather Lucas had already made the decision to give her the new identity so he had them give her a new face at the same time. When the doctor removed the bandages covering her face, she went into hysterics. She was kept under sedation for three days."

Reid clenched his fist, wanting something to pound it into—a wall, Lucas, anything to make the pain go away.

"Alicia couldn't have gone back to being an agent anyway, Reid," Mari cried out. "To this day the thought of going back out into the field sends her into a cold sweat. Back then she thought of her work as some kind of game, a dangerous one, but still a game. She learned differently and she knew then she couldn't take it any more. Lucas convinced her to take up a new life and she did just that." She pressed her fingertips against her lips. "And you went on with your life, Reid." She attempted a light-hearted laugh that didn't quite come off. "After all, it didn't take you long to find someone when you were in Mexico, did it?"

"I didn't find just someone, I found *you*," he

grated. "Ironically, I found the same woman I was there to let go of. You have always been in my heart. I didn't expect to throw you out but I knew it was time to go on with my life. Little did I know life would play such a macabre joke on me."

"You were there to let go of Alicia," she corrected. "And you met Mari. There's a big difference."

"No, there isn't!" he shouted. "You're the same woman, and I wish you wouldn't refer to Alicia as if she no longer exists."

Mari stood up. "She doesn't exist any more," she insisted, holding out her hands. "Don't you understand? For over three years I have had to convince myself that Alicia is dead. You don't understand what it's like—the nights where dreams are dangerous, where you're afraid to go to sleep in the dark for fear someone might attack you, where you wake up in a cold sweat and run to the mirror to make sure you're still in one piece. Then to look in that mirror and see a face you don't even recognize, and you have to stand there and tell yourself that you're not going crazy." It was evident by the stiff way she held her body and the bleak expression on her face that Mari still suffered from horrors he wouldn't be able to understand in a thousand lifetimes.

"Alicia used to write letters to you in her head," Mari said so softly that Reid wasn't sure he had heard her correctly. "She was afraid she'd go insane unless she did something so she wrote you what prison was like, her dream of escaping, even though she doubted it would happen, and her hopes for the future." She stared out the window, trying to gather up her inner strength before she broke down completely. She had to get away before she lost control. "I think I'll take my shower now." Without looking back at him she walked out of the room.

Reid ached to pull Mari into his arms and will the pain away. His head was spinning with Mari's story. Actually, Alicia's story. Damn, he didn't know what to call her any more. He raked his fingers through his hair wishing an easy solution was around the corner but he knew that wasn't possible. Hell, nothing made sense!

At least he now knew why Lucas tried to get him out of Mexico and why Thorson had so much trouble finding her file. He smiled grimly. He doubted Lucas was very happy with him. He probably knew now that Reid had tracked Mari down.

Reid knew he would have to come to terms with what he'd just heard. And there was no better time to begin than now.

Mari tried a hot shower in an attempt to ease the tension from her body. She had managed to hold on to her composure until she stood under the water. It was then that her body convulsed and painful sobs tore from her throat. She finally leaned against the tile and allowed the agony to wash over her.

"Hey." Reid's voice murmured in her ear as he stepped into the shower and gathered her in his arms. "You know I could never handle tears."

"All we're doing is hurting each other." She

sobbed, hanging on to his shoulders for support. "If his men find you they'll kill you in some horrible way and I couldn't bear that happening, knowing it would be my fault. Please, just go and forget everything I told you. Get as far away from me as possible."

He stood so that she was sheltered from the shower spray. "No way, my love. We've had these years stolen from us and I don't intend to lose any more time. We'll work this out together."

"Work what out? Don't you understand, he's still after me!" Mari cried out.

Seeing that wild look in her eyes again, Reid hustled her out of the shower and dried her off before steering her into the bedroom. After settling her on the bed, he sat beside her with his arms tightly surrounding her.

"There's no way he can find you," he assured her. "It was purely by accident that I found out the truth, and even then I probably wouldn't have if I hadn't pushed it."

"They already know."

Reid stilled. "Why are you so sure?"

"Remember that day we went to the temple? Someone was there and called for Alicia, taunting me. I pretended to ignore it, but I don't know if the man believed me. Then I received a phone call asking for her," she explained. "I told the man he had the wrong room and I can only hope I sounded convincing. I just don't think so."

"And your room was trashed," he mused. So the man on the bus had been following her, not him.

215

No wonder he wasn't on the bus going back and there were no confrontations while he was there.

"And I recently received a box of flowers, dead flowers," Mari continued dully.

Reid covered the side of her face with his palm, pressing her cheek against his chest. He wanted to make love to her so badly he ached. Instead he rained tiny kisses over her face, murmuring assurances that she wasn't in this alone and that no one would ever hurt her again. He also vowed silently that if he ever met up with the man called Black Death, he would kill him slowly and very painfully. Reid would make him suffer the way he made his woman suffer.

Mari calmed under Reid's gentle ministrations. She hadn't felt this safe in a long time, but soon feeling safe and comfortable wasn't enough. She didn't want a flurry of light kisses, she wanted his mouth, hard and hot, possessing hers. She didn't want his hands soothing away her fear; she wanted the deep penetration of his body into hers, the act that truly made them one. She turned in his arms and settled her mouth on his. Her hands were bold in their quest. She felt a familiar heat building up in her body, beginning at her feminine core and radiating outward in strong waves.

"Mari, you've been through too much," Reid murmured. He was afraid that loving her the way he wanted to would bring on another attack of hysterics.

"Heal me," she demanded in a throaty voice that was a combination of Mari and Alicia. "Make me whole again, Reid. I want to feel you inside of me, performing that special magic." Her hand circled his velvety hardness and stroked the pulsing shaft. "Give me life."

Groaning, Reid pulled her onto his lap. His tongue plunged deep into her dark secrets, seeking out all she had to give while his hands covered her breasts, kneading the swollen globes.

There was an intensity to their lovemaking that hadn't been there before. They were two lovers who had lost each other only to be reunited under unusual circumstances. Their hunger ran unchecked as they demanded more and more. They couldn't get enough of each other.

Reid declared his intent to taste every inch of Mari's body and he did just that. He suckled at each breast and his fingers rolled the nipples into dusky-pink pebbles aching for more of his touch. He moved down to the smooth skin of her belly and tickled her navel with his tongue as he murmured how soft and sweet-smelling her skin was. He smiled and listened to her pleased moans when his mouth settled over that part of her that ached so deeply for him.

Mari was convinced that she had died and gone to heaven as Reid's tongue and nibbling lips sent her off to that galaxy far far away. She gasped and arched upward under the hot brand of his mouth.

"I need all of you," she pleaded, grabbing his shoulders. "Now!"

He looked up and grinned. "Whatever the lady wishes." He moved over her, entering her in one smooth deep thrust. Mari automatically wrapped her legs around his hips, her fingers digging into the taut skin of his buttocks. She moved rhythmically under his driving thrusts. There was a primitive taste to their lovemaking as they both strained to reach that pinnacle. Reid wasn't about to let it happen too fast. At one point he put his arms around Mari and rolled over so that she was on top. He kept his hands on her hips and controlled the pace until she took over. Her skin glistened like wet silk, her lips swollen moist and pink from his kisses, her eyes wild, not with fear but with desire. She dipped her head, taking his lower lip between her teeth and nibbling on the soft inner skin. She felt her breathing constrict, her body seemed to swell as the heat built up to an unbearable level.

"I can't go on." Each word seemed torn from her. She threw her head back, her teeth bared against the pleasure pain surrounding her in volcanic waves.

"Yes!" Reid hissed, his own features contorted with the effort of holding back until the last possible moment. And that moment was fast approaching.

When it came they were both ready to fly to the heavens together. The sky seemed to open up and rain down fiery colors as they moved faster and faster and their voices shouted with the love they had always shared.

Mari collapsed onto Reid's chest, breathing deeply to fill her tortured lungs.

"It has never been like this," she whispered, combing her fingers through the wet hair on his chest.

His hands ran up and down her bare back. "No,

but I'm not surprised. After all, we're making up for more than three years. No wonder you felt so right that first time." He nuzzled her throat, inhaling the womanly scent of her skin.

"If I recall, you were probably down there looking for a blonde," she couldn't help teasing. "And in fact, you found one. Just the kind you always appreciated."

He winced, recalling the sophisticated Carole. He was relieved to see the terror gone from Mari's eyes and laughter making them sparkle again. "So I took a nice little detour before I found the real thing. Just remember, *you* were the one I went to bed with."

If Mari could have found an ounce of spare flesh on his body, she would have given him a nasty pinch.

"I could have murdered you and torn her hair out by its black roots when I saw the two of you together," she admitted softly. "And then that first time you kissed me and called me Alicia I was so jealous I saw red. I went back to my room and threw the tantrum of all times when the person I was jealous of was actually me. Ironic, huh?"

"It appears I knew what I was doing even then." He settled her more comfortably against him. "Hey, what can I say? We've always been a great team, in and out of bed, especially in."

Tears sprang in Mari's eyes. "We can't stay together, Reid. That would be more than enough evidence for Black Death that Alicia was alive, and he would certainly come after the two of us. I don't want your death on my hands. If anything happened to you. . . ." Her voice failed at even the thought of losing him forever in such a final way.

Reid hugged her tightly. "Nothing is going to happen to me," he said firmly. "And I'm certainly going to make sure nothing happens to you. I lost you once. I won't lose you again." No, he wouldn't lose her again. Nothing short of death would separate them again, and the way he felt he would even fight the devil himself to keep him and Mari together. Funny, he knew the woman he held in his arms was the woman he fell in love with years ago and that her true name was Alicia Brookes, but he now thought of her as Mari. Perhaps she was right, after all. She wasn't Alicia any more and couldn't be. What had all of this done to her mind? It showed she was a much stronger woman than he imagined and he couldn't help but love her more.

Reid looked down and noticed that Mari had fallen asleep. She looked so fragile that he was afraid to move for fear of waking her. From the way she talked, that nightmare was a fairly regular occurrence. His eyes darkened with anger at the man who was most at fault for this. From now on Reid would handle any future problems with Lucas. In fact, he would make a quick trip to D.C. to have a long talk with Lucas about Mari and the death threat hanging over her head.

Moving very carefully, he edged his way out of bed and moved over to the window that faced the front of the house. Barely breathing, he looked out and saw an unexpected sight. Across the street was a nondescript sedan with two men sitting inside. Ten to one they were Lucas's men. Well, he would just have to give them something to report, wouldn't he?

CHAPTER ELEVEN

"Do you have plenty of food in the house?" Reid asked idly, munching on cheese puffs, part of their impromptu meal that evening along with hot dogs and French fries. He had let Mari sleep while he prowled the house, eager to learn her new lifestyle.

"I have a deep freeze in the cellar filled with meat and vegetables and a well-stocked pantry so we won't starve, if that's what's worrying you," she replied, wondering what was going through his mind. "When I feel depressed I grocery shop."

He grinned. "Then I'm glad you've been depressed because I think we'll hole up here for a while."

"Hole up? In case you don't remember, I have a business to run," she argued, although the idea of being alone with Reid for days on end sounded very enticing.

"You have an assistant and a clerk to run your shop," he pointed out. "There's no reason why you can't take off a few days. I think Denise would expect it after yesterday. Will you call her and ask if she'll take charge?"

"I just got back from a vacation!"

"So, take another one." He turned serious. "Besides, I'd like this chance for us to get to know each other all over again."

Mari contemplated her hot dog. "There's more to this than our getting reacquainted."

Reid nodded. He stood up and held out his hand. Mari took it and allowed him to lead her into the small den adjoining the living room. He stayed her hand from switching on a light and led her over to the window.

"Be very careful when you look outside so you're not seen," he advised quietly.

Mari barely moved the drape as she looked outside and saw the same car that Reid had seen earlier.

"Lucas." She confirmed his suspicion. "I called him after I received the dead flowers and he promised me protection." She looked up at him. "That means he knows you're here. I'm surprised he hasn't called to chew us both out."

He grinned. "He might have. I'm sure he's tried to do just that, but I unplugged all the phones so we'd be assured our privacy."

Mari reached up and kissed him lightly. "Oh, how I love a man who thinks on his feet," she breathed.

He pulled her harder against him. "Lady, you better love me for reasons other than that," he warned.

"I don't think you have any worries on that score. You seem to think very well off your feet too."

Since it wasn't very late, Mari called Denise and asked if she would take over the shop for a few days. Denise easily guessed the reason why and was only too happy to help out.

Reid then suggested that they watch an old movie on TV in the den with all the lights off so they could neck.

It was the first evening that Mari didn't spend an hour or two in the exercise room and she didn't miss it one bit.

"Isn't this a nice way for us to get to know each other all over again," Reid asked as they lounged in the Jacuzzi late that night.

Mari had rested her neck against the edge, her eyes closed. "Mm, perfect." Her toes nudged his lap.

He chuckled as he caught her foot in one hand. "You're a new woman now and I have to learn all about her. You were the one who told me that Alicia is gone." His eyes dimmed for a moment. "So I guess I should find out about Mari."

Her stomach muscles tightened. Obviously he didn't realize what all that involved.

"For a time I didn't feel like Alicia or Mari," she told him. "If anything, I felt more like Frankenstein's daughter. I had some kind of heavy bandage on one leg because I had torn some ligaments, my face was completely bandaged, and I drank my meals from a straw for so long that to this day I can't stand to look at one. The days ran together so much I didn't know one from another.

I later learned I was in the clinic for almost four months."

Reid again thought very seriously about killing Lucas. She had been all alone in a medical clinic where no one gave a damn about her as long as her blood pressure and temperature were normal. What had happened to her wasn't right.

"Why were you there for so long?" he asked quietly.

"They wanted my face to heal completely before I left the clinic." She smiled wryly. "How my mother survived her times with the plastic surgeon I'll never know. The first time I saw my face I saw two black eyes and a few fine-lined scars. In time the scars pretty much disappeared. They don't show at all now when I wear base makeup, but then every centimeter was so sore I didn't dare touch myself for fear everything would fall apart." A faint sparkle lit up her eyes. "Oh, Reid, even you would have left the country if you had seen me."

He massaged her foot, bending the toes back and forth and listening to her groan of appreciation. "You said you had to be sedated when you first saw your new face."

The sparkle left Mari's eyes. "Oh, yes. That was a day I doubt I will ever forget. Lucas had come in with flowers. That alone should have warned me something was up. I doubt he even sends his mother flowers on holidays. My ultrasensitive nose almost died from the perfume so they were taken out immediately. The doctor seemed very agitated as he snipped the bandages. I later learned that Lucas had given orders that I not be told about my new appearance. All I had been told was that my cheekbones and nose were broken and needed some repair work. So when I was handed the mirror I figured I'd be looking at the old me, with maybe a few changes. Instead I saw an entirely new face. I asked if this was some kind of macabre joke and when Lucas didn't say anything and the doctor looked uncomfortable, I knew there was nothing funny about it. I started laughing and screaming and didn't stop until they sedated me." She shook her head, wishing to rid herself of those memories. "I think the idea of having more medication upset me more than anything. You see, I was in so much pain while recovering that I became afraid to take too many painkillers for fear of becoming addicted. Let me tell you, it would have been so easy since I was allowed a pill just about any time I wanted one. I decided after a while to live with the pain. That was how I knew I was alive," she said simply.

Reid closed his eyes, swearing under his breath. "Why?"

"Lucas was playing God. Who knows what goes on in his head? I think he figured he could have a brand-new agent without worrying about all the training. The trouble was, he soon learned that he had a broken-down agent who went crazy every time the word assignment came up. The idea of going out into the field sent me into hysterics. I lost it."

Reid knew exactly what she meant. All of them worked under so much pressure, and the realization they could be killed any day was just another cloud over their horizon. There were many agents who couldn't take the pressure more than a few years and then either took a desk job or got out of the work altogether. The agency's medical benefits covered psychological help, and it was used a great deal. "Losing it" meant that agents just couldn't handle the work any more and had to get out before they went crazy or were killed or, worse, caused someone else to be killed by accident.

"You said you couldn't retrieve the information you carried in your head," he commented.

Her features tightened. "Lucas asked for it several times in the beginning but trying only brought on violent headaches. The psychiatrist he had me see explained that it was a psychological block and I wasn't going to give up what he needed until I felt safe again. Naturally Lucas had another, more graphic name for it, but he had no choice but to back off. That was when he sat down and had that little heart-to-heart talk with me. Before that I had no idea why the new face or why you hadn't been in to see me. Lucas would only tell me that you were out of the country on assignment. Of course, I had trouble believing him because I knew you would have contacted me in some way." Her voice faltered and he hurt with the pain he had inadvertently caused her. "Lucas explained that Black Death's group didn't believe I was dead and that there was a contract out on my life. If they found any proof that I was still alive, they would hurt anyone who was dear to me, namely my parents and, most especially, you."

That was when he exploded. "And you believed him?"

"Of course I did!" she cried, shifting on the bench. "I was recuperating from injuries that left me feeling very vulnerable and unsure. I also knew what Black Death was like. Reid, he isn't a man, he's a killing machine. Pain and agony make him happy. He used to call me the blond princess and promised to turn me into a hag. If I had stayed in that prison much longer I'm sure I would have been just that."

Reid hesitated, hoping that he had the tact to ask this question properly and praying that he wouldn't hear the answer he didn't want to hear. "Did he ever make sexual advances toward you?"

If Mari hadn't been crying she probably would have laughed. "He didn't want sex! He just wanted to watch your blood flow and your face contort with the pain he caused. There was a rumor he was impotent. I heard there were other women incarcerated in the prison but I never saw them. I also heard they were given to the guards when he was finished with them. They usually died not long after." She spoke matter-of-factly as if discussing the weather. So much of the emotional pain she had suffered during that time had been buried so deep she still treated it as if it had happened to someone else. This was the first time she unconsciously admitted she had been the one there and not used Alicia as a shield.

Reid inhaled sharply. He had been taken prisoner only once. He had a cigarette burn on his thigh as a result, but he had been able to escape before more happened. He wasn't even sure he could have survived all that Alicia had and remained sane. No wonder Mari took the chance of a new life offered to her. He certainly would have. It was probably why she shied away from him in Mexico. He was a reminder of an old life, one that had to be forgotten, and the only way she could do it was to stay away from him.

"So you promised Lucas to give up your family and me?" he asked quietly.

"I had no choice. If any of you had died as a result of me I wouldn't have been able to live with myself." She ducked down until the water lapped around her neck to dispel the chill surrounding her despite the hot bubbling water she sat in. "I worked very hard to turn into Mari Chandler, who was the exact opposite of Alicia Brookes. And I'm not just talking about the accent or gestures. I had to think like her too. When I felt comfortable enough with my new persona, Lucas assisted me with funding for my shop and setting up my new past. Then I got on with my life."

Reid couldn't help but wonder jealously who else might have helped Mari to get on with her life. He had been assuming that she had remained relatively solitary, but . . .

"And does Mari have a full social life?"

Mari's head snapped up at the harsh note in his voice. "What you mean is, how many lovers has she had over the years?" She stood up and climbed out of the Jacuzzi, grabbing a towel along the way and wrapping it around her.

Reid practically leapt out of the spa and ran after her, grabbing her arm and pulling her around to face him. "Yes, I mean lovers," he said roughly. "How many men have known you the way I have? I remember Alicia very well. She could be insatiable at times, although I admit she was very discriminating about men and she was faithful to me as long as we were together."

Mari jerked her arm free. "Damn you! Alicia is dead!" she shouted. "And my past love life is none of your business. I doubt you've been revering Alicia's memory over the years, have you?" She noticed the red tinge along his jaw and correctly guessed the reason. Without thinking twice, Mari swung her arm and slapped Reid in the face as hard as she could then turned away to leave the room as quickly as possible. She was angry but she was smart enough to know that she had just made him furious and she was wise to get out of his way as quickly as possible.

But Reid was faster. He grabbed her arm and spun her around. She could see the white prints from her fingers on his skin and the dangerous glint in his eyes. Oh, yes, he was furious. She had neatly turned the tables on him. He was more furious at himself than at her but she was the only thing he could take his anger out on that moment. He threaded his fingers through her hair and pulled her head back, gratified to see anger in her eyes instead of fear.

"There may have been a few sexual interludes

230

in my life during the past three years but that was all," he informed her harshly. "I hadn't made love to a woman until I met this cute little thing named Mari Chandler, and I made love to her because she stirred something in me that had been long dead. Now, if you can't handle that I don't know what else to say."

"After being with you all other men paled in comparison," she whispered. "I didn't even want to try. Oh, I knew the time would have to come for me to take a lover, because I didn't want to be alone for the rest of my life, but I was afraid that my identity might be revealed at any time and I'd have to go into hiding again. And there are my nightmares to contend with. It wasn't fair to ask any man to have to live with that."

Reid's grip on her arm lessened. He remembered his and Alicia's talk about a family, the children they would have, a large dog and a station wagon to haul the kids to Scout meetings, dance and music lessons, and Little League. Alicia may have looked like the perennial social butterfly, but she wanted more than attending all the right parties and polo matches and in loving Reid she had found it.

"Why can't I stay angry with you?" He groaned, closing his eyes in pain.

"Because you love me?"

That simple phrase was enough to drive him to his knees. Yes, he did love her. He loved both women, Alicia and Mari, and was able to recognize them as two separate people, but why didn't that seem enough for him?

"Go to bed," he ordered wearily.

Mari looked at him with concern. "Aren't you coming?" Oh, God, he wasn't going to leave now, was he? She didn't think she could bear it if he did.

He shook his head. "I have some thinking to do. I'll be there later, I promise."

She nodded and left. If he promised to come to bed, no matter how late it would be, he would come.

Mari washed her face and brushed her teeth automatically. She took a shower and slipped on a nightgown before climbing into bed. It seemed so large and lonely. But then it always had, until last night when Reid had occupied a very important part of it. She punched her pillow and rolled it up to fit her neck as she curled up on her side where she could see the bedroom doorway and the night-light flickering on her dresser. She could hear the faint click of metal striking metal upstairs. Reid was making use of the exercise equipment. It was a long time before she fell asleep listening to the sounds of weights clinking together.

Hours later Reid, damp from a recent shower, slid into bed and gathered a sleeping Mari into his arms.

"Reid?" She roused long enough to identify her late-night visitor.

"Go back to sleep." He feathered a light kiss over her lips.

"You didn't turn off the night-light, did you?" she mumbled.

He chuckled. "No, I didn't. Why?"

"S'good. Have nightmares if no light." She

drifted off before he could ask her why. Then he remembered the previous night and what she had babbled about—the dark cell, the fear of rats. Was that why she needed a light? So if she woke up she could reassure herself that she was safe and not back in that hellhole?

Reid couldn't remember bouncing over so many emotional tracks as he had in the past twenty-four hours. And Mari had only told him a fraction of what had gone on! He damned Lucas for sending Alicia to the Middle East when she obviously hadn't been prepared for such a dangerous assignment. And where had her backup been? No agent goes into a dangerous situation like that without a backup. Lucas just pounded another nail into his coffin.

The next morning they watched the sedan leave and another take its place.

"I should be flattered," Mari commented. "He has two agents keeping an eye on me twenty-four hours a day. I hope they're getting paid overtime for this."

"How do you know they aren't here to make sure I'm safe?" Reid teased, then pretended pain when she punched him in the arm.

She shook her head. "I can't see this as a game, Reid," she said quietly. "So much has happened that I can't laugh about it any more."

He somberly agreed. "You can't go back to your store, Mari. If that bastard is out there looking for you he just may try to pick you off."

"He doesn't want to kill me," she replied with chilling certainty.

Reid spun around. He didn't like the sound of her voice. "Why do you say that?"

She smiled wanly. "Woman's intuition. He's furious that Alicia made a fool out of him by escaping and quite possibly living to tell the tale. He has an extremely keen mind and an evil one. Now he is thinking about his vendetta toward her. If he finds her again he will take her back to his prison, and there will be no escape for her this time."

Reid felt the surrounding air choking him. She believed what she was saying! What was worse was that he believed her too, and he feared for her. How many years had their agency been after Black Death? It had to be at least six, maybe seven, and the man had only been known for eight years.

It hadn't taken the terrorist leader long to become known for his waves of cruelty upon the country's innocent citizens. The agency alone had lost several agents to the man's group. He had always been clever enough that no one saw his face and lived to tell the tale. Wait a minute, *no one?*

"What does he look like?"

Mari lifted a shoulder and shook her head. "He always stood in the shadows, or I was forced to wear a blindfold. His face is still a secret. That was one of Lucas's first questions to Alicia when she was able to talk. Black Death is very clever in making sure no one sees him. That way he remains a mystery and hopes to keep people more fearful of him."

Reid nodded in understanding. "Like Alicia." It was a statement, not a question.

Her eyes blazed. "You're damn right she's afraid of the man. She had good reason to be. He left her with a fear of the dark that she may never recover from and nightmares that will probably haunt her for the rest of her life." She ran her fingers through her hair in an agitated gesture. Her face was pale, her eyes bright with unshed tears—tears Alicia had never been able to shed while she was in prison because that would have meant she had given up, and that was one thing she refused to do.

Reid drew her into his arms and held on to her tightly. He found himself wanting to protect her. Mari was afraid and now so was he. He was scared to death that if he left the house something would happen to her, but he would have to leave sooner or later. His planned confrontation with Lucas had to be done face-to-face in order to be effective.

"Please get out of this, Reid," Mari cried, burrowing her face against his neck, her tears anointing his skin. "I couldn't bear it if anything happened to you. If he killed you I'd die too because I wouldn't have anything to live for."

He grabbed her by the arms and shook her hard. "I don't want to hear that kind of talk," he ordered. "You survived the past three years and so did I. We found each other again, and I'm not letting you go, Mari. We're going to see this through together and then we're getting married and having those children we planned so long ago."

"You planned those with Alicia!"

"We're also going to merge your dual personality once and for all."

"I told you, I have to think like that in order to live a sane life. Even the doctor couldn't help me come to terms with what had happened. He finally said it was something I would have to do myself."

Reid's face was taut with the deep feelings he had for this woman. He cursed the doctor for not being willing to take the extra time needed to help her come to terms with what she had been through. "If you have nightmares, I'll be there to chase them away," he vowed. "If you need a night-light to sleep, so be it. I'll keep the lights on in the entire house all night so you won't have to be afraid. Nothing, and *no one*, is going to hurt you again. I love Alicia and I love Mari, it doesn't make any difference who you are."

"I'm not a skinny blonde." She sniffed.

He ran his hand tenderly over her hair. "It isn't hair color or the body shape that I love, but the woman inside. In the beginning I couldn't understand why I would just look at you and want to make love to you. Now I know why. No matter how hard you try to fight it, you're essentially the same woman. Mari had to hide Alicia to keep her safe. She saw Alicia as all that she wasn't, but deep down, no matter how much you deny it, Mari and Alicia are still the same person."

She shook her head violently. "You're not the one who looks in the mirror every morning and wonders who she's seeing," Mari argued. "You're not the one who has to remind herself who she really is."

"So what do you intend to do, run for the rest of your life? Are you going to ask Lucas for a new identity and hiding place?" Reid's face whitened when he saw the guilt written on Mari's face. "That's exactly what you were going to do, wasn't it? Why?" he demanded.

"Because there's nothing else I can do!" she shouted. "I can't allow other people to die because of me!"

The sane part of Reid's mind noticed how she again acknowledged herself and Alicia as one person, but he was too far gone in his anger to care. He wanted to shake some sense into her. He also wanted to love her so deeply that she would never run away from him again.

"You're right about not being the same person any more," he said finally. "Alicia never feared anyone or anything."

"That was because she hadn't met anyone or anything to be afraid of until she entered that prison," Mari retorted, jerking away from his grasp.

Reid closed his eyes and visualized the woman he had known three years ago. Shoulder-length blond streaked hair, those maddening purple eyes, saucy grin. He opened his eyes and saw chin-length brown hair, green eyes . . . that was what was wrong. His hand shot out and gripped her chin, forcing her to face him.

"When are you going to remove those damn contact lenses?" he commented sardonically, staring into her eyes and observing the curved disks floating gently.

"Not until the time I'm supposed to take them out."

"Take them out."

Mari stiffened. "They're only taken out once a month. This isn't the time to do it."

"I don't give a damn whether it's time or not. Either you take them out or I will." He needed to see the true color of her eyes. He needed to see all of the woman he always loved.

Mari still hesitated. The lenses had been an integral part of her for the past three years. She was used to having green eyes. The grim look on Reid's face told her he meant what he said. She slowly turned away and put her hand to one of her eyes. A green disk dropped into her hand. The mate popped out a minute later. She raised her head and for the first time Reid was able to look into eyes that altered between a deep midnight blue and purple according to her mood. Now they were very very purple. He inhaled sharply.

"All you'd need is the blond streaks," he murmured, twisting her face from one side to another.

"I'm not Alicia any longer," Mari bit out each word, freeing herself from his grasp. "I'm me, Mari Janette Chandler, of Charlotte, North Carolina. When will you get that into your thick skull? I can't go back to the person I once was. I worked too hard to get where I am."

"What about your parents?" he asked quietly. "Don't they deserve to know what happened? To know you're still alive?"

She sighed heavily, lowering her head. "Tell me the truth. Would it be better for them to know the daughter they thought they had lost three years ago is alive after all? And what if something happened to me next week or next month or next year? Why should they go through that pain again when they don't have to? Reid, I don't like this any more than you do, but I've had to give up a lot too, and you seem to forget that. When I sat in a corner of that hellish hole called a jail cell I was convinced I wasn't going to come out alive. But I was determined to remain sane to the end. I named the rats Larry, Moe, and Curly and endured the never-ending bugs. To this day I can't look at a spider without shuddering. I was always hungry because the food they gave me wasn't fit for a dog. Now I believe I've told you pretty much everything. All the scars on the outside have been erased by a very competent plastic surgeon, but I still carry scars inside from those months. I only ask one thing of you: Alicia is dead, please, just let her be," she requested in a weary voice.

Reid knew Mari was right. Oh, he might want to argue against her decision from now until doomsday, but he was aware that Alicia's—correction, Mari's—life had changed over the years. He was more than a little disgusted with himself. She had gone through hell three years ago and was going through some dark times now and he wasn't helping her very much by bullying her.

"Let's make some coffee," he suggested. "And didn't I see a cheesecake in the freezer?" Mari nodded. "Then let's defrost that and have it with the coffee. This time I promise that I'll listen while you talk."

Ten minutes later they sat on the couch in the den, Mari snuggled close to Reid, his arm wrapped warmly around her shoulders.

"I really don't have anything more to say, Reid," she told him quietly, burrowing her cheek into the hollow between his shoulder and neck. "Please understand that the past month has been very traumatic for me. I went to Mexico to release you from my soul so I could go on living. I had no idea you would be there. Lucas found out and ordered me out. I told him that I had had to give you up three years ago, and while I wasn't going to tell you the truth, I was going to take what I could."

"Good for you," he approved heartily, pleased she had been brave enough to stand up to the strong-minded Lucas.

"But I also told him that I would leave you when the time came," she went on. Reid didn't appreciate hearing that half as much. "I was afraid to make love with you because I felt I would give myself away."

"In a way you did. There was that moment I felt as if I had come home." He dropped a kiss on top of her head. "And obviously I had. What my eyes didn't see, my heart did."

"Oh, Reid, that's a beautiful thing to say," Mari murmured, rubbing his chest with her palm in a circular motion. "After we made love I was afraid you would want answers that I couldn't give, so I ran."

"And you didn't think I would follow you?" He was incredulous.

"No, I thought you'd see me as a ditzy flake who didn't deserve another moment of your time and you'd say good riddance to me," she admitted. "I hoped you would see me that way because I knew we couldn't have more."

"Wrong." He leaned forward to grab his cup of coffee and sip the dark bracing liquid. "We can have a great deal and we will, just as soon as this problem is settled."

"Reid, we're not talking about some petty criminal, we are talking about one of the most feared terrorist groups in the world," Mari argued. "This is my problem, not yours."

He laid his fingers against her lips to silence her. *"Our* problem. I intend to fly up to D.C. day after tomorrow to see Lucas and learn all I can about this. You're not going to live in fear another day, Mari, and when this is all over we're going to pick up where we left off. There will be no more splitting us up and Lucas won't be sending me off anywhere." He correctly anticipated her argument. "I'm not leaving you, and you're not running away from me again."

"This is a very old subject."

"Maybe so, but if I have to repeat this old subject for the next fifty years I will." He lowered his head to brush his lips over hers. "And if I have to make love to you for the next fifty years to convince you of my intentions, I will happily do so," he murmured, biting down on her lower lip with delicate intention. "Now, do we watch the eleven o'clock news or do we go upstairs so I can begin on my campaign?"

Mari decided to wait to read the morning paper to find out about any current events.

CHAPTER TWELVE

Mari didn't sleep well that night. Several times she crept out of bed and peeked out the bedroom window to watch the sedan parked across the street. Once she saw an orange-red spark, obviously a match held to a cigarette before it was quickly extinguished.

She had been trying to ignore the feeling of doom she had been experiencing for the past few hours. Her skin felt tight and her nerve endings raw—just the way she used to feel before something bad happened during an assignment.

She prowled the house, looking out each window, but found nothing to feel suspicious about until she looked out over the backyard and the woods beyond. She couldn't see anything wrong but not seeing anything didn't mean her enemy wasn't in the vicinity.

During the past few hours Mari had come to two conclusions: She wasn't going to fall back into Black Death's hands like a grand prize and she wasn't going to run away and hide either. She had run enough and in the end she lost her family, her former life, and the man she loved. Now that she had found him, she refused to lose him again.

Her mind made up, Mari's brain raced with ideas. She knew the first thing that had to be done was to get Reid out of harm's way. Oh, he had told her he was going to Washington, D.C., but she knew he would return that same day if possible. She couldn't have him coming back so soon, and there was only one person who could help her.

Mari slipped downstairs to the kitchen. She reconnected the wall telephone and dialed a number. She listened to the varied clicks until her call was connected to the proper party.

"Yes?"

She didn't hesitate now. "I want Reid taken out of here."

"When?"

"In the morning."

"He won't be happy."

"That will be two of us, but it has to be done. I also want the other one caught, and I'll do anything possible to ensure it." She could sense his smile of satisfaction.

"Everything will be taken care of. Have your front door unlocked before eight A.M. I'll take it from there," Lucas assured her.

That was what Mari was afraid of. "I don't want Reid hurt," she warned him. "I just want him taken somewhere safe until this is over." And then she would be free to love him the way he deserved to be.

"It will be done. Now listen to me carefully because I want you to follow my instructions to the letter. With luck this will be all over within forty-eight hours." He spoke swiftly and after ascertaining that Mari understood, he hung up abruptly.

"And good-bye to you too," she said wryly, hanging up her phone.

Her plans made, Mari went back to bed. She slipped under the covers and into a sleepy Reid's arms.

"You're cold," he mumbled, running his hands over her naked body.

"Then warm me," she encouraged throatily, trailing her fingers through the crisp hair on his chest and down to his hips.

Reid needed little inducement. He moved over her, slipping easily between her parted legs to rest in the feminine cradle of her hips. His mouth coasted over hers lightly then returned to deepen the kiss. His tongue flicked out to touch her lower lip, withdrew and touched it again, this time slipping inside with the lightest of caresses.

"More," Mari whispered, sliding her arms around his neck to pull him closer. At that moment she needed him more than anything. It was fire touching fire and no amount of water could banish the flames roaring between them.

"In time," he whispered back, continuing his teasing caress. "I'm too busy enjoying the feel of your beautiful skin." His lips fluttered over her face like a flock of butterflies. One hand moved down to cover her breast, warming the cool skin until it felt hot to the touch. His thumb rubbed the nipple in a loving rasp that sent electric shocks to the center of her womb. His mouth found the pulsing vein in her throat and felt every heavy beat pounding against his lips. "Just looking at you any time, night or day, is enough to turn me on."

"Even when I wear baggy jeans and a sweatshirt?"

"Yep, and especially when you wear nothing." One hand briefly investigated her femininity and found her moist and throbbing for him.

"You're trying to drive me crazy." She moaned, using the same pleasurable punishment tactics on one of his flat brown nipples that peaked instantly at her touch.

"I'm just beginning." Reid's tongue investigated the tiny hollow at the base of her throat and over to where her shoulder met her collarbone. He then lowered his head to bury his face between her breasts. "You always smell like the spring," he muttered, running his tongue over the swollen curve and up to the pouting nipple. Every inch was bathed lovingly by his mouth and tongue.

Mari closed her eyes, easily imagining what Reid was doing to her. She swore she could hear her blood singing in her veins. He was having no problem warming her up. When his hand cupped her warmth and pressed inward, she hooked her thigh over his, silently asking for more.

His answer was to roll onto his back and pull Mari on top of him. She smiled as she raised herself up to straddle his hips and then lowered herself onto him.

Mari wanted no gentleness from him. She needed to be wild, to get caught up in a storm of forgetfulness. This was one night she would carry in her heart for a long time because she feared once Reid learned that she was the one to have him taken away, she just might lose him again no matter what happened. If she had to lose him, she would, just as long as she knew he was alive.

All too soon they had to return to earth. Mari collapsed on Reid's chest, her own chest rising and falling heavily in an attempt to bring air into her lungs.

Reid lay still, stroking Mari's tangled hair. He couldn't remember feeling anything so primitive as the moments they had shared before. He lifted his head when he felt something warm drop onto his chest. He ran his forefinger over Mari's cheek and found it damp.

"You're crying," he mused, surprised she would have tears after such a beautiful sharing of bodies and souls. "I couldn't have been that bad, could I?" He attempted to joke her out of her sudden sorrow.

She shook her head. "No, they're tears of happiness," she lied, wiping her eyes with her fingertips. "Everything is so perfect I just hate to have it end."

He chuckled. "Oh, baby, this isn't going to end, this is only the beginning for us. We're going the whole nine yards this time. When I go up to D.C. I intend to hand in my resignation." He held up his hand for silence when she opened her mouth to protest. "No arguments, I've been thinking about getting out for a long time now. It's better I get out while I'm still in one piece. Then we'll look into that two-story house with the white picket fence and a dog in the backyard. Hell, I'll even buy you a station wagon," he joked.

Mari just wanted to cry even more. Yes, everything was perfect now. Too bad that cloud's silver lining was going to tarnish first thing in the morning.

A few minutes before eight, Mari unlocked the front door while she went into the den on the pretext of checking on their bodyguards. She wasn't surprised to find the car gone. If these men knew Reid at all, they would be aware that he wasn't going to be any easy captive.

Reid watched Mari cook breakfast in a more haphazard way than usual. She had already broken two plates. She was upset, he didn't need to be astute to see that. He would have inquired what was wrong but he doubted he would receive a truthful answer. He could only wait and see what had upset her.

Mari could barely eat her bacon and eggs. Her nerves were raw waiting for the sound of the front door opening. She began to wish she hadn't called Lucas; she wished Reid hadn't tracked her down; she wished she wasn't wanted by a master criminal. There were a lot of things she wished but they weren't going to get her anywhere. She was going to have to live with this day by day, hoping it would be over soon and that Reid wouldn't hate her when it was.

"Reid?" A male voice intruded abruptly.

His head snapped up at the sound. Three men wearing light-color suits stood in the kitchen doorway. Reid turned to Mari.

"It appears we have company," he drawled before turning back to the men. "Hello, Tom, you came a long way for nothing. I was flying into D.C. tomorrow to see Lucas. You can tell him so when you go back."

"We came for you, Reid," Tom said quietly, keeping his eyes on Reid's relaxed form and knowing the other man was ready for battle.

"Then you're wasting your time."

The three men stood a short distance from each other in a semicircle watching Reid the way a hawk watches a chicken except in this case it could very well be the other way around. Reid was equally watchful. He glanced at Mari and noted her white features. She didn't appear very surprised to see their unexpected visitors.

"What is going on here?" He directed his question to her.

"Just go with them, Reid," she said quietly, looking down at her clenched hands lying on top of the table. "I don't want any trouble, please."

Reid frowned. There was something very wrong here. "Tell me, Mari. What's going on?"

She couldn't say anything.

Tom approached Reid, who had stood up by now. Reid's stance was that of a man prepared to fight and inflict a great deal of damage. But he couldn't watch all three men. Before he knew it his arms were jerked behind his back as he tried to kick out and strike Tom.

"Lucas promised he wouldn't be hurt!" Mari cried out, jumping to her feet.

Reid's head snapped around, his eyes blazing

249

with anger. "You did this, they're here because of you," he accused.

Mari knew she would have to play a convincing role if she didn't want Reid to fight these men. She straightened up, her eyes clear although not very calm, and her features smooth as glass.

"I have work to do and I can't do it with you here," she told him in a cool voice. "The past few days have been fun but it's time for all good things to come to an end."

Reid looked at her with cold hatred. "There were some men who used to claim that Alicia was a cold bitch. She had nothing on you." He tried to free himself from the man's grip. "Don't worry, I'm not going anywhere," he assured Tom. "Except to get the hell out of here."

Tom shook his head. "Orders."

Mari watched the four men walk out of the room. Tom turned to give her an apologetic look but Reid didn't say another word or glance at her. She may have saved his life but she had lost him in the process.

When the men reached the car, Reid stopped short. "Wait a minute," he mused. "Something's wrong here. She wouldn't—" He didn't get another word out as Tom quickly bared Reid's arm and injected him. Reid was out immediately. Tom turned around to see Mari standing in the doorway looking miserable.

"He's fine," he assured her as the other two men stuffed an unconscious Reid into the car's backseat. "It was a precaution in case he didn't go with us peacefully. We wanted to avoid trouble at all costs."

Mari turned around and closed the door behind her. She couldn't bear to watch them drive away. She carefully locked the door behind her and leaned against it, listening to the engine start up. She felt very frightened of the future. Lucas had said that with luck it would be all over in forty-eight hours. The trouble was, there was no guarantee she would be alive then. She wasn't afraid of death, she had lived with it hovering over her head for too long; but she wouldn't welcome it with open arms either.

Within an hour, all the telephones were reconnected, the breakfast dishes washed and dried, and she had showered and dressed. Mari sorted through Reid's clothing and did several loads of laundry.

The waiting was the hardest part, but there was no guarantee when she would be contacted. It would depend on how long it took for the revised information to reach the proper ears.

As the hours passed, Mari convinced herself that she had made a mistake. This wasn't going to work and she would end up with the raw end of the deal.

How could she have been so stupid? she raged at herself as she worked out in the exercise room.

Why did she think this would work? she asked as she made the bed, inhaling Reid's scent lingering in the sheets. She was tempted to replace them with clean ones so she wouldn't have any reminders of him around her but she couldn't bear to do it. She needed the slightest hint of Reid with her for courage, because she still had none of her own.

How could she have listened to Lucas's crazy plan? she cried silently as she sat before the television not seeing one thing on the screen. Nothing mattered but getting this over with as soon as possible. She was so lost in her thoughts that when the telephone rang she jumped in her chair. She covered her pounding heart with her hand as she reached for the receiver. Was it going to happen already?

"Hello?" She wished her voice didn't sound so husky and unsure.

"Everything has been taken care of." For once Lucas's crisp voice calmed her instead of upset her.

Mari didn't say anything, she wasn't expected to. She replaced the receiver in the cradle and sat back in the chair, her knees drawn up to her chest and her arms wrapped around them. It was too late to back out now.

Reid woke up with a cotton taste in his mouth and a pounding head. "Damn!" He swore, sitting up and holding his aching head with his hands.

"I see you're awake." A steaming mug was held in front of him.

Reid accepted the cup of coffee from Tom. "How long have I been out?" He sipped the strong brew with a grateful sigh.

"About sixteen hours."

He swore again. That meant he could be anywhere in the United States. Knowing Lucas, he wouldn't be surprised if he had been taken out of the country altogether.

"I would have preferred knockout drops in my scotch over that damn hypo," Reid grumbled, finishing his coffee in an attempt to wash the metallic taste from his mouth. He settled back on the cot, his hands clasped behind his head and legs crossed. He may have looked relaxed and at ease with the world but Tom knew better. He had known Reid for well over ten years, but he freely admitted he still didn't know everything about him. Right now, he did know one thing—as far as Reid was concerned, Tom's life wasn't worth a plug nickel.

"So what's the plan?" Reid's voice was friendly, his smile casual, but his eyes were cold gray chips.

"We stay here for a while."

"May I ask why?"

Tom looked apologetic. "You can ask but I can't tell you."

Reid shook his head. "Was this Lucas's idea or Mari's?"

Tom remained silent.

"Fine, let me guess. Mari was stupid enough to worry about my safety and asked Lucas to get me out of the way. That's where you and those two goons you brought along came in. And she's sitting there as prime bait." His eyes glittered with dangerous lights. He straightened up. "Damn you, she could get killed!" he shouted, leaning forward.

"Reid, she has protection," Tom assured him. "Every precaution has been taken to keep her safe."

Reid thought of other times when precautions had been taken but they hadn't meant a damn thing in the end.

"Want something to eat?" Tom asked. The dark look Reid sent him was answer enough. Tom backed out of the room, locking the door behind him.

Reid looked around the small room, which was obviously part of a regulation safe house. The windows were covered by shutters fastened on the outside and central air conditioning hummed through the vents keeping the temperature comfortable. He knew the adjoining bathroom would contain nothing to aid in an escape. The furniture was minimal—a narrow cot, a chest of drawers, and a chair.

All the comforts of home, he thought wryly.

He focused on the idea of getting out as soon as possible. He checked his pockets and found them picked clean. Even the knife he carried in a sheath strapped around his calf was gone. They were certainly thorough. Now it was time to think about Mari.

He knew what was going to happen and he wasn't going to allow Mari to go through it alone. And when this was all over, he just might strangle her himself! For now he'd just rest and clear his mind of the drug. He was going to need all his wits about him when the time came for him to escape. He sat on the hard cot listening to the men murmuring in the other room. He knew that someone would always be on duty throughout the night.

He'd just have to choose the right time for his escape and hope that he was at least still in the U.S.

Mari was in a state of acute nerves before midnight. She had spent the evening cleaning out her closet, rearranging the linen closet, and working on the store ledgers. But none of that helped ease her tension. She just wanted all of it to be over and done with. She wouldn't even have minded if Lucas had called her. She was just grateful Reid was safe. He was probably very angry with her, and that anger could linger a very long time. That hurt the most. But she could live with it as long as she knew Reid would be alive.

She wrapped her robe closely about her, but she still couldn't get warm. The cold was deep in her bones. She doubted she would ever get truly warm again.

She wasn't startled this time when the phone rang. She picked it up and spoke coolly. "Yes?"

"I know you are alone, Alicia." The voice from her nightmares filled her ears. She grabbed the receiver with both hands.

"I'm sorry, you must have the wrong number." Mari spoke with an icy calm.

That maddening chuckle sounded cold and evil. "Oh, no, my dear, that line won't work any longer. I have proof you are Alicia Brookes. It is very late now. I suggest you get your rest. Time is growing short because I wish us to be together again soon. Until then, my darling."

Mari remained glued to the floor long after she heard the *click* of the broken connection. Her hands shook badly when she set the phone down. Her first impulse was to call Lucas. Had he set up the tap? Was someone watching the house right now? What about the woods? Were they covered too? She choked back a sob. Just as suddenly that earlier icy calm returned to invade her body. He had suggested that she sleep so she may as well do just that. Nothing was going to happen tonight.

Mari undressed and put on a nightgown. She huddled in bed, staring at the night-light and reliving every time she and Reid made love. She held his pillow against her chest for comfort the way a child holds a teddy bear. As she slipped under the covers she tried to tell herself that she wasn't alone in this, but it wasn't very easy to believe.

Reid had the ability to set an alarm clock in his head. He decided four A.M. was a safe hour and settled back to sleep until then. When he woke up, he called out, asking for the dinner he'd earlier refused.

"You're a regular bastard, Reid," Tom announced, entering the room carrying a tray twenty minutes later. "By all rights I should make you wait until breakfast."

"Hey, you wouldn't starve an old buddy, would you?" Reid placed the tray on his knees. He looked at the contents and grimaced.

Tom stood back a few feet and watched Reid closely. He wasn't about to relax around the man because he knew just how quick Reid's reflexes were; after all, they had gone through basic training together. His orders from Lucas were to keep Reid out of the way until further notice, and he didn't intend to screw up this assignment.

He looked disgusted when Reid, once finished with his meal, "accidentally" dropped his tray.

"Give me a break, Reid," he grumbled, stepping back another foot. "That trick is one of the oldest in the book. Pick it all up and do it slow."

"Okay." Reid dropped down on one knee and gathered up the plate, coffee cup, and utensils, preparing to put them back on the tray. In a flash, the tray connected with Tom's face and the man buckled at the knees. Reid's clasped hands hit him on the back of the neck and Tom was out cold before he hit the floor. Reid quickly looked down the hallway, both ways, prepared to fight his way out. Obviously the other two were sound sleepers. He grinned. Lucas wouldn't be too happy to hear that his men could sleep so soundly with a prisoner in the house. He took the time to rifle Tom's pockets and grab a ring of keys then he closed the door, locking it behind him.

Reid heaved a silent sigh of relief to find his belongings on the coffee table in the living room. He crept outside. Although one of Tom's keys fit the car ignition, the motor didn't turn over. After a swift look under the hood, he found the rotor missing—their idea of safety in case he did escape. Not wanting to take the time to look for it, he disconnected the battery cables and tossed them into a nearby field to make sure they couldn't follow him. Then he threw the keys as far away as possible and took off in the opposite direction.

Why do most of the safe houses have to be in the middle of nowhere? he asked himself as he loped down a rocky path in search of a house, town, anything. He was hoping that he was still in North Carolina or at least within a decent driving distance.

It was a very long time before he came upon a farmhouse. He slipped around to the back where he found an ancient beatup pickup truck parked behind the barn. He checked the license plate and was relieved to find it registered in Virginia. He held his breath as he hot-wired the ignition. When the engine sputtered to life, Reid straightened up and shoved it into gear.

As he roared down the road, he saw a man, wearing a pair of long johns, running past the gate carrying a shotgun.

"Bring back my truck, you son of a bitch!" the man yelled, lifting the gun to his shoulder.

Reid swore under his breath as he gunned the engine, praying it would get him out of range in time.

As he bumped down the road, he checked the gas gauge and swore again. Barely a quarter of a tank.

"Terrific, I'm going to go to jail for stealing a car that probably won't even get me to the next town," he muttered.

A quick search of the glove compartment turned up a map and the truck's registration. Hm, it was probably a six-hour drive to Charlotte. He wasn't as far away as he had feared. He only hoped the truck would survive the several hundred miles and that he wouldn't get picked up by the police. The way the past twenty-four hours had gone for him, getting arrested would be the highlight of his day.

Mari woke up several times during the night and turned over searching for Reid's comforting warmth, then wanted to cry when she remembered why he wasn't there. She got up and roamed through the house, looking out windows, but saw nothing. That didn't make her feel better. Were only her enemies out there or were Lucas's men lurking in the shadows too? She wanted to laugh. Wouldn't it be funny if they ran into each other? Maybe they could compare notes on the latest spy techniques during their prowls. Did spies on the loose like this take a coffee break? She sighed. If she was thinking sick jokes like that, she deserved to get caught by Black Death.

Lucas called Mari late the next morning.

"No one has been seen near your house so far," he told her. "But, as you know, that doesn't mean anything. Do you have any idea what may happen next?"

Mari was surprised that he would ask her opinion when he usually preferred giving his own whether wanted or not.

"I think it will happen tonight," she said slowly, trying to think past the dark curtain closing off the section of her mind that dealt with her other life. "He's toying with me, wanting me to break down. He might even want me to make a run for it so he can pick me up on the road and spirit me away before anyone knows what has happened. He enjoys the element of surprise, but he also likes to play with his victim's emotions. With me he'll do both and much more." There was barely a quaver in her voice.

That night, while she lay awake, she thought a lot about those never-ending days and nights in prison. Had that time broken her as much as she feared, or had she just needed this time for healing? If she was still afraid of what might happen, she wouldn't have allowed herself to be used as bait. Of course, she might have still carried that fear if it hadn't been for Reid. It was the thought of his presence surrounding her like a warm blanket that kept her sane throughout the long dark hours of waiting for the axe to fall.

Before that happened she had one more thing to do. She went into her office and sat at her desk with a sheet of stationery in front of her. If anything happened she wanted to leave something behind for Reid.

My darling Reid,

There is so much to say that I don't know where to begin. I could remind you of that wonderful night we spent in Budapest or our weekend in Paris or even that week in Geneva. Instead, I'll talk about now.

The days we've spent together have been heaven. You are heaven. For the past three years I have been living an empty life. How empty I hadn't realized until we met again in Mexico.

I now have something to live for: You and the

260

*future we can have together. I don't want you to
hate me for what I did. Please believe that I did
it for you, just as I'm doing this for myself. It is
time to put all those fears behind me and I have
to handle this myself.*

*No matter how much you shout and swear at
me for doing what I did, I know I was right in
this.*

*I intend to be present when you read this
letter. If for some reason I am not, please remember how much I love you.*

*All my love,
Alicia*

She folded the sheet twice, slipped it carefully
inside an envelope, and sealed it before writing his
name on the front. Mari pressed her lips against
the envelope and placed it on the desk before
turning out the light and leaving the room. The
time for her to meet the enemy was growing close
and she wanted to be prepared mentally as well as
physically.

CHAPTER THIRTEEN

It wasn't long after midnight when Mari woke up in a cold sweat.

He's here! she thought wildly. *He's here.*

She slid out of bed and dressed quickly in black jeans and a black sweater with a dark windbreaker over it. Keeping the lights off, she went downstairs to the cellar.

At first glance it looked like any other cellar. She moved to one side of the furnace and lifted a lever set into the wall. A door slid silently open to reveal a completely equipped gun room. She smiled at the idea of keeping a secret from everyone, including Lucas. When Mari had bought the house the owner had shown her the room, explaining he had been an avid collector but had lost interest over the years. She decided to buy the guns although she had no idea they would come in handy.

Mari headed for the handguns, choosing a lethal-looking Luger. She screwed a silencer onto the barrel. She knew it had the kick of a mule but a sore arm was preferable to becoming a sadist's prisoner. She loaded the gun, put several clips in her jacket pockets, and looked around to see if there was anything else she could use in her defense. It wasn't that she didn't trust Lucas's men to protect her, but she knew how Black Death worked. During those months in prison she had observed the man, had listened to others talk about him and filed the information in the back of her mind. It may have been buried deep in her subconscious these past years, but now since it was so badly needed it floated upward. The only way she was going to win was to keep reminding herself that she was now strong enough to beat him at his own game.

Mari left the outside floodlights off as she slipped out the kitchen door, locking it behind her. She wanted everything to appear normal on the outside. She sensed he would be in the woods, but the idea didn't frighten her. She had walked them almost daily, knew them as well as anyone. There was a large pond a mile away; she walked there during the spring and summer to watch the ducks frolic on the water. And there was an old treehouse not far from there. She guessed it had been a boys' clubhouse years ago. Since her only neighbors were away on vacation, any gunshots wouldn't be heard or reported. That wasn't good, or perhaps it was, since Lucas's men should be out here somewhere too.

Mari skirted the woods and stopped by the first stand of trees. She took several deep breaths, reminding herself that she was doing this in order to be free of the nightmares and fear, and she immediately felt much calmer. She pulled a pair of thin black leather gloves from her pockets and put them on.

The adrenaline was flowing through her veins. The longer Mari stood there the more psyched up she felt for this adventure. Oh, yes, it was an adventure—one that belonged to Alicia. After all, it was due to her this dangerous tryst was taking place.

"It was always a game to Alicia, a dangerous game, but a game nevertheless. She didn't realize what really happened in this business until that time she spent in prison."

This game has new rules now, she thought grimly, searching the velvet darkness beyond her for the slightest movement. Winner take all.

Mari crept from tree to tree, stopping to look in each direction. She didn't see anything, but she wasn't going to rely on just the one sense. She strained her ears to hear the slightest sound, a leaf or twig crackling, a rock skittering, anything. She even sniffed the air for the scent of after-shave or men's cologne. Sooner or later something would give someone away. Lucas had told her all of his men would have blond hair, explaining that that was the best he could do for her by way of identification. It was enough.

Strangely, Mari didn't feel alone. There was too much going on in her mind. Reid was talking her every step of the way.

Shadows can be your enemy. Watch them, know them as well as you know the back of your hand. They can also be your friend when you're the one who needs to hide.

*Your gun doesn't have to be in your hand every
minute but make sure it's where you can get it at a
second's notice. And that means no hiding it in
your bra or the waistband of your pantyhose!*

*Keep your emotions under wraps, Alicia. That's
one way you'll stay alive. Never let anyone know
exactly what you're feeling. Always keep them off
guard.*

With Reid's voice guiding her every step of the
way, Mari moved farther into the woods.

If Reid knew he was so helpful to Mari he might
not have worried so much when he discovered
that the truck wouldn't go faster than thirty miles
an hour on the highway. He alternately cursed
and begged the vehicle to speed up, but it was
elderly and temperamental and it refused to listen
to any of his pleas or curses. He had stopped once
to smear mud on the license plates to hide the
incriminating numbers before he halted to fill up
the gas tank once again; it appeared to be a gas
burner. He worried when he found the attendant
listening to the radio, but the old man didn't look
at the truck once as he took Reid's credit card.
Reid had to stop several more times after that, as
the engine was giving him trouble.

Reid thought once of calling Lucas, but he figured the man would just send someone else after
him and this time he might not be so lucky. All he
could do was pray that he got to Mari in time. If he
didn't, well, then there would be even more
bloodshed because he wasn't going to allow Black
Death to get away again.

* * *

Mari hid behind a tree, taking silent shallow breaths. This man had dark hair and carried an Uzi. She had few choices. She could shoot him and hope the silencer would muffle the shot enough that no one else would hear it. She could remain in her hiding place and pray he didn't find her. Or— or what? Her few choices turned out to be two. She opted for the latter. This was not the time to show her hand.

From her vantage point she saw a man's figure bend over the lock to her back door and enter her house. She was relieved that she had gotten out when she had.

The other man had stopped and lit up a cigarette. Mari rolled her eyes. She decided he was an amateur. Didn't he realize how far the tiny light could be seen in the dark of night? Black Death was surely slipping if he brought along idiots like this one. She broke out in a cold sweat just thinking of that name, but she quickly roused herself. This was not the time to fall apart. Not if she wanted to remain alive and yes, she did want that. She wanted to see Reid again, to hold him in her arms and love him.

She stiffened when she heard a low-pitched harsh voice. It was clear that someone had come upon the man taking his cigarette break and he wasn't happy about it. Mari wasn't sure what he was saying but the tone indicated that he ordered the man to extinguish his cigarette and get back to looking for her. She hunched down to make herself as small as possible, listening to the crunch of

266

leaves underfoot as they walked away. When she felt they were far enough beyond her, she crept away.

Every taut nerve in her body told her she was going to have to face Black Death, whether he was captured by Lucas's men or not. She swallowed the bile in her throat. The dark memories associated with him were frightening. It was going to take every ounce of courage for her to go through with this. The thought of her being forced to return to that hellish prison if she lost this battle was enough to keep her going on.

She was glad she knew the woods so well. She knew where each hollowed-out tree was, the location of the infamous treehouse, and she was aware that it had been built sturdily enough to hold her weight if need be. Except she couldn't hide out forever. She took several calming breaths and thought back to Reid's lectures when they first began working together.

Always do what they don't expect you to do, he had told her. *If they think you're going to act rough and tough, pull the poor-helpless-female on them. Or the other way around. Just so you keep one step ahead of them.*

That's what I'm trying to do, Reid, she thought to herself, crouching behind a bush as her eyes scanned the foliage for the least movement. He expects me to sit cowering in my house waiting for him to capture me. Hopefully he doesn't have any idea that I called Lucas, and he thinks I'm here alone like the proverbial sitting duck. If he's acting arrogant he might also end up careless, and that's what will aid me. I'm not the quivering woman he turned me into three years ago. I'm not! With that declaration in mind her earlier fears disappeared.

Her eyes grew cold with resolve. The fear was gone and her adrenaline was pumping again. She had been a victim once, she wouldn't be again. She only hoped Reid would understand why she did what she did and forgive her for it when this was all over. She saw the outlines of two men standing near the pond. It might not hurt to check them out. Remaining in a crouch, she crabwalked parallel to the path leading to the pond.

Reid stopped the truck several hundred yards down the road from Mari's house. He stepped out and made his way up to the front door. All looked quiet but that meant nothing. He tried the door and found it unlocked. Cursing softly, he carefully opened it and slipped inside. Standing very still, he listened for the slightest sound. He knew right away that Mari wasn't in the house. He would have sensed it if she had been there. Ah, a footfall overhead, and it was much too heavy to be Mari's. It might not be a bad idea to investigate. He was angry at her and he was ready to vent it on the first person he found.

He had a good idea that Lucas's men were around. Lucas might be a bastard, but he would protect her. Especially if it meant he could catch Black Death for his personal trophy. That meant that whoever was lurking upstairs could be friend or foe. Reid was determined to capture first and ask questions afterward.

Reid found the unwanted visitor in the bedroom. Acting fast, before he could raise an alarm, Reid jumped sideways and lashed out with the bottom of his foot, catching the man in the chest. He was unconscious by the time he hit the floor. Reid hurriedly tied him up using several of Mari's silk scarves and another for a gag. He picked up the gun and hefted it in his palm.

"Freeze!"

Reid's head snapped up at the same time the gun lifted in a firing position. Only the fact that he recognized the man standing in the doorway prevented him from shooting.

"Good way to get killed, Morgan," the man drawled, lowering his gun. "I thought you were out of commission."

"I'm sure you did." He glanced down at his prisoner. "Yours or theirs?"

The man looked down. "Nope, all of our men here are blond. Lucas wanted to make it easier for Mari to identify them. We already found two others not far from here and have them in custody."

Reid swore. "Where is the son of a bitch?" Meaning Lucas.

"Right here."

Reid's superior stood behind the other man, his eyes as cold as ever. "Tom called me a short while ago. He is very embarrassed about your escaping."

"Hey, he didn't think I would do anything," Reid admitted with a cocky grin. "There's no reason to send him off to Siberia. By the way, I had to steal a truck to get here so if you don't want me picked up for grand theft auto I suggest you take care of that little matter. The truck is parked down the road."

Lucas said nothing. Reid didn't have the power to surprise him, no matter what he did. "Have you seen Mari?"

Reid shook his head. "I was just going to ask you." His face hardened into a granite mask. "Don't you realize her fear of this man could get her killed?"

"Or banish her nightmares forever by having to face him."

Reid didn't believe that but he wasn't about to argue the point just now. He pushed past the two men and hurried downstairs. Mari was outside, he knew it. For some crazy reason she had gone out there alone and he had to find her. He turned around.

"If anything happens to her, Lucas, I'll kill you," he grated.

Reid's mind was racing. There was something that nagged at him as he thought of an unprotected Mari out there alone. Or was she unprotected? He ran downstairs and into the kitchen and from there to the cellar door.

He found the light switch at the top of the stairs and turned it on. When he reached the bottom he looked around. He remembered when Mari had shown him around the house. There was something out of place down there but he hadn't gotten a chance to ask her about it, not when all he could think about was taking her back upstairs to bed.

There it was, the suspicious lever to one side of the furnace.

"What have you found?" Lucas asked, coming up behind him.

"I'm not sure." Reid pulled the lever and watched the wall open slowly. "Well, well, well," he murmured. "A regular armory. Mari, my love, you're full of surprises."

"Why didn't I know about this?" Lucas demanded, surveying the various rifles and handguns.

"Probably because she needed to keep at least one secret from you." Reid picked and discarded several handguns. When he found one he liked he rummaged around for ammunition. He thought about taking a rifle also but didn't want the extra weight to slow him down. He dropped extra clips in his pockets and turned back to Lucas. "Whether you like it or not, I'm going out there after her."

"This operation is very important to us, Reid," he warned. "Don't blow it just because your hormones are thinking instead of your head."

Reid pushed past him. "Oh, I'm sure you'll get your man, Lucas. I'm just going to make sure it doesn't cost anyone's life to accomplish it," he grated, running back up the stairs. "Don't worry, if I see anyone with blond hair I promise not to shoot."

He sneaked out the back door and flattened himself against the house's brick exterior. Would she have gone into the woods? he wondered. Going there was her best bet to keep safe.

Stay calm, honey. He hoped she believed in mental telepathy. *I'm coming.* He pushed away from the wall and found his way to the edge of the woods, hoping he would find her before anyone else did.

Mari remained frozen behind a tree near the edge of the pond. It had been so easy! Actually, too easy. The man she had learned to hate three years ago was standing no more than a hundred yards away and she could hear every word spoken.

"She is here," the man called Black Death told his subordinate. "I can feel her very close to me." He laughed, the dark laugh of Lucifer. "Aren't you, Alicia?" He spoke louder. "I know you are near me, my darling. You couldn't stay away for long, could you? I missed you."

The fear was back. It clawed upward from her vitals to her throat. She would have been violently ill if she hadn't forced herself to think clearly. There was no way he could know she was there, she told herself. She had showered before she had gone to bed and hadn't put on any scented powder or cologne so she couldn't be given away due to feminine vanity while standing downwind of the enemy.

"You forget all those hours we spent together." Black Death spoke. "Come to me, Alicia. We have so much lost time to make up."

As if she had been hypnotized, Mari stepped away from her hiding place. She held her gun up, one hand cradling the other to keep her aim steady.

"Not again." She was pleased that she didn't sound frightened even though her entire body was screaming. "This time you're the victim." She spared a glance at the man near him. "Tell him to put his gun down, very carefully."

He smiled and uttered something Mari couldn't understand. The other man also smiled. Within seconds his gun flared, but he was the one who fell to the ground. Though Mari was quick enough to evade his shot, he wasn't fast enough to evade hers.

"Very good." Black Death applauded, still standing at ease, not looking the least bit frightened that her gun remained pointed at him. "My little girl has grown up."

Mari lifted her chin, staring at him with cold eyes. "Your mind games won't work any longer. I'm going to kill you. Now, toss your gun into the pond."

His handsome savage features remained impassive. He didn't seem to worry that he might be dead at any moment as he pulled a pistol from inside his jacket and threw it into the water.

"Ah, I miss the loveliness of your blond hair. You were the most beautiful woman I had ever known. I only wish we had met under other circumstances. Perhaps we could have become close friends then."

She was pure ice standing there with the moonlight washing over her. "Spare me. It was common knowledge you don't like women except as victims." It took every ounce of strength to keep her aim steady.

He shook his head. "You can't kill me, Alicia. To hurt me is to hurt yourself. I know how to make

273

the pain go away just as easily as I brought it on. Remember?"

To her horror, the barrel wobbled just the slightest bit. Black Death's keen gaze didn't miss her momentary weakness.

Reid had heard the shot and feared what it might mean. He took off at a run in what he hoped was the right direction while praying he wouldn't find Mari lying in the dirt. Judging by footsteps not all that far behind him, he guessed he wasn't the only one to hear it; he just hoped they would be in time. He skidded to a stop when he reached the knoll overlooking the pond and gazed down at the deadly tableau before him.

The man down there had to be Black Death. No one else would stand that confidently in the face of a gun. And it was Mari standing there holding that gun. Reid knew the look on her face. She may look brave on the outside but she was scared to death. Sometimes being frightened was a good thing to be but not now; not for Mari.

"No-o-o!" he shouted, but the strong breeze carried his plea off in the opposite direction. Reid was afraid to go down there for fear any movement would distract Mari and cause her death. He could only stand there and pray all would be fine. He cursed himself for not bringing a rifle. The Colt he carried was good but it didn't have the range he so desperately needed now.

For a moment Mari only saw a gray haze before her eyes. When it cleared she was certain that Black Death had moved forward several steps. He was going to overpower her if she didn't do something fast! Her entire body was aching with memory. Yes, he could make the pain go away, but he also created it and she never wanted that again.

"Give me the gun, Alicia," he coaxed, holding out his hand.

"No," she croaked, stiffening her arms, but he didn't stop walking toward her! Keeping her eyes on his arrogant smiling face, she slowly pulled the trigger.

When Reid saw the gun fire he took off with the speed of light. By the time he reached Mari, Black Death lay writhing on the ground, screaming insults and curses at her.

"Reid!" she cried, throwing her arms around him and hugging him tightly, afraid he was a figment of her imagination.

"Are you all right?" he demanded, running his hands over her body and her damp face to make sure she hadn't been harmed. His hands slowed when they returned to her face. Groaning, he held her so tightly she thought her ribs would break, but having him back in her arms was worth the pain.

She laughed shakily, her fingertips finding the dampness on his cheeks. "My love. You were with me the entire time."

He didn't stop to question her meaning. He turned to the man who had stolen his woman from him so many years ago. He saw the wound in Black Death's thigh pouring blood onto the ground and wished it had been higher.

"You bitch!" he screamed, holding his leg with

both hands. "I'll get you for this." His savage features turned to Reid. "Do you honestly want this woman after what I've done to her?" There was no mistaking the sexual implication.

Reid's face hardened. "You're lucky I know you're trying to throw me off balance because otherwise I'd kill you here for even implying that."

He turned to Mari and grinned cheekily, draping his arm around her waist and pulling her against him. "It appears he can't take what he dishes out."

Mari collapsed against him, burrowing her face against his throat. "I was so frightened," she whispered. "But I knew I wasn't going to let him take me away from you again. It was the thought of you that kept me going."

He squeezed her gently. "Don't worry, no one is going to take you away from me again," he vowed. His gaze hardened when Lucas and his men appeared. Lucas gestured for two of the men to take Black Death into custody.

"Who shot him?" he asked the couple.

"Mari," Reid said proudly, then added grudgingly, "It appears you were right. She faced her fears and fought them bravely."

Lucas nodded. "I'm not surprised. You taught her well a long time ago."

"You'll have my resignation on your desk in the morning," Reid announced. "I've had it with the spy games."

Lucas chuckled. "You'd be bored within a month."

Reid shook his head as he steered Mari back to

the house. "Wanna bet? I'm going the whole nine yards—the white picket fence, two-point-five kids, the dog, and the station wagon along with Little League and ballet lessons."

"I have a proposition for you two," Lucas called out, following them.

Mari looked up, thinking the worst. Reid assured her with a smile and a quick kiss.

"No thanks," he called back. "We have some talking to do. Good-bye, Lucas."

"This isn't the end, Reid," Lucas shouted. "We'll talk about this when you're not thinking with those damn hormones."

They didn't acknowledge him as they walked back to the house.

"Think you can put up with a beat-up old spy for a husband?" Reid asked as they walked upstairs to the bedroom. He was relieved they had carried out the other man and there was no trace of a struggle there. He'd explain about the missing scarves later. Right now he preferred thinking with his hormones.

Mari's eyes filled with tears. He didn't hate her for what she had done to him after all! "I'm sure I can put up with you for at least a hundred years." She choked, throwing her arms around his neck.

"One minute." Reid left her and ran back downstairs. When he returned he was grinning broadly. "I just wanted to make sure the locks were secured. I don't intend for us to have any more unwanted company right now." He swept her up into his arms and carried her over to the bed. In moments he had her stripped very efficiently and discarded his own clothes.

Fear was one of the greatest aphrodisiacs known to man. Mari clutched Reid's back as he entered her with one deep thrust. Their bodies moved and strained as they strove to touch the highest reaches of life. After the horrors of that night, it wasn't long before Reid shouted and poured himself into her. Mari lay back gasping for air, running her hands over Reid's sweat-slick back.

"I didn't think I could do it, Reid," she confessed later when they lay curled up spoon fashion. "I didn't think I could shoot him."

"But you did." He brushed a strand of hair to one side and kissed the vulnerable curve of her throat.

Mari felt secure in Reid's arms, felt secure they would be together for always, but there were still things to talk of.

"I may have faced him but that doesn't guarantee the nightmares are over," she told him quietly. "And I'll have to remain Mari Chandler."

"Mari Morgan," he corrected. "I wouldn't care if your name was Brunhilda as long as you stay with me for always. I told you before, I'm going to help you fight it. Tonight you faced the man who has haunted you for years. After that, the rest of the battle is going to be a snap."

Mari wasn't so certain it would be that easy but she didn't speak her doubts aloud. Reid sounded so sure that she was willing to feel confident for his sake. They turned their heads when the telephone rang.

"I'll give you three guesses." Reid groaned, picking up the receiver and speaking before the caller had a chance to say a word. "No, Lucas, I don't care what your lame-brain idea is, I am not interested. Find another errand boy." He slammed down the receiver and then took the precaution of pulling the cord out of the wall jack.

"He won't give up, you know," Mari mused, smiling as Reid returned his attention to brushing kisses all over her face. "Lucas doesn't want to lose you and he isn't going to if he can help it."

"Fine, let him keep trying. That doesn't mean I'm going to listen or go along with him." He moved up and over her. "Not when I have a honeymoon to plan. Want to help?"

"How do you plan a honeymoon?" She flicked her tongue over her lower lip.

"Easy, by trying out everything to make sure it works," he said, moving over her once again.

Mari laughed throatily. "Yes, my love, it appears everything works just fine," she murmured as she gave herself up to the pleasures he had planned for her.

EPILOGUE

Mari sat at her desk and gazed over the report she had been trying to read for the past hour.

"Hey, wife, it's quitting time." Reid's voice floated over her head just as he swooped down to place a lingering kiss on her lips.

"None of that." She batted playfully at his wandering hands. "The last time you got smart we shocked the secretary."

He grinned. "Why do you think I automatically lock the door when I enter your office now?"

Mari leaned back in her chair as Reid perched himself on the edge of her desk. "You look very smug," she teased.

He nodded. "Any time I have a run-in with Lucas and come out the winner, I feel extremely proud of myself. We'll have another therapist on board within the next month."

She chuckled. How well she remembered those dark days almost two years ago when she had faced her greatest fear. Black Death now languished in a federal prison. Apparently his hold over his group wasn't as strong as he had thought since another man took charge the moment hi arrest was known. Then there was Lucas trying to talk Reid and Mari into working for him again. They both refused until Mari heard his plan.

He didn't want them back in the field. He was astute enough to know that Mari would never be able to handle that, but she was perfect for something else. Lucas had talked to several other agencies and one thing they agreed on was a need for some sort of halfway house for burned-out agents. And who better to run such a house than one burned-out agent and another who had worked under the pressures in the field and understood agents' needs?

Mari wasted no time. Ironically, Denise bought the shops and had done well as owner even though she still protested she wasn't management material. Mari then enrolled in several psychology courses and insisted Reid do the same. With the same fervor she had in starting her shop, she had thrown herself into setting up the house they found in Maryland.

She and Reid had married almost immediately after Black Death's capture, and she couldn't have been happier. Reid had done all that he promised. He was always there to help her fight the nightmares and make her feel safe and loved. He even assisted her in finding another therapist and attended as many of the meetings as he could. He was determined to know all he could to help her. It had taken time, but she had even come to terms with the fact that she and Alicia were the same person no matter how hard she had tried to separate them.

They also talked about a family—in fact, Mari had thrown away her birth control pills just the month before. They knew they had much to work out before having children, and the last two years had taught them a lot. Now it seemed like the right time to begin their two-point-five children, as Reid enjoyed saying.

Reid looked at Mari with eyes filled with love. She had given him so much during the past years. They spent their honeymoon in Mexico; it seemed the fitting place, and when Lucas talked to him about his plan and Mari chipped in her own two cents, Reid knew he didn't have a chance. He was going to do whatever she felt was right and this was most definitely right.

In their work they helped men and women enter real life and taught them they didn't have to live in the shadows of the night any longer. And that not every stranger they met was necessarily a stranger. Some took longer than others and there were some failures, but Mari and Reid never stopped. While they weren't certified therapists, they did understand the pressures of the job and with what Mari had gone through in prison, they could easily identify with the many fears an agent suffered.

"How about an early dinner and an early night?" he suggested quietly.

"We have an early dinner and early night just about every night unless we have an emergency here. I swear, after two years of marriage you're still a sex fiend," she teased him.

"So I'm consistent." He leaned forward to capture her mouth. How he craved the taste of her! Two years hadn't diminished his hunger for this woman who leaned into his kiss and put her arms around him. If anything, his need for her intensified as time went on. He was also very proud of her. For the first time last night Mari had asked that the night-light not be turned on and she had slept the entire night through. Reid knew this wouldn't happen every night. If Mari was overtired or had a stressful day the nightmare might very well come, but he loved her for trying. He pulled back his head and studied her face. Her eyes were shining and her lips were moist from his kiss.

"You know," he said huskily, feeling the same deep emotion he had always felt with her, "I'm very glad I decided to go to Mexico when I did."

"So am I," Mari whispered. "Even more so, I'm very glad you decided not to take up with that blonde. I do so hate violence but I meant what I said a long time ago. I would have torn her to pieces."

Reid laughed out loud as he pulled her out of her chair and dropped into it himself, drawing her into his lap. His hand unbuttoned her blouse and slipped inside to find the peaked nipple that he knew was a dusky rose in color and tasted as sweet as honey. His other hand slipped under her skirt to find the lacy edge of her panties above the scalloped band of her thigh-high hose. She certainly knew how to drive him crazy. He had watched her smooth them on that morning and all day he had fantasized taking them off.

"Few people get a second chance the way we did," he said quietly and with a solemnness Mari wasn't used to.

"And for that we will always be thankful." Mari clasped his head with her hands and brought his mouth back to hers. At that moment she could have cared less if the door was locked or not. They could always get another secretary who wasn't easily shocked by co-administrators who couldn't keep their hands off each other.